The Witches of Blackthorn Hollow

Samantha Hill

Published by Samantha Hill, 2024.

THE WITCHES OF BLACKTHORN HOLLOW

First edition. August 29, 2024.

Copyright © 2024 Samantha Hill.

ISBN: 979-8227614117

Written by Samantha Hill.

Introduction: In Memory of the Women Persecuted as Witches

Between the 16th and 18th centuries, England was gripped by a fear that led to one of the darkest chapters in its history—the witch hunts. The Witchcraft Act of 1542, passed by Parliament, defined *witchcraft* as a crime punishable by death. Although this Act was repealed just five years later, it was reinstated by a new law in 1562, further solidified in 1604 under King James I, a monarch deeply obsessed with demonology. The 1562 and 1604 Acts marked a significant shift, transferring the trial of accused witches from the Church to the ordinary courts and setting the stage for widespread persecution.

Formal accusations against those labelled as predominantly poor witches, elderly women, reached a peak in the late 16th century, particularly in the southeast of England. During this period, 513 individuals were put on trial for witchcraft between 1560 and 1700, with 112 of them meeting their deaths at the gallows. The last known execution for witchcraft in England occurred in Devon in 1685, and the final trials were held in Leicester in 1717. In total, around 500 people in England were executed for witchcraft, victims of a society consumed by fear and superstition.

The witch hunts in England, much like those across Europe, were fueled by ignorance, misogyny, and a fervent desire to root out perceived evil. These trials were not just about the belief in magic; they were also a means of controlling and punishing women who deviated from societal norms—those who were independent, knowledgeable, or simply vulnerable. The accused were often subjected to horrific tortures to extract confessions, and the trials themselves were rarely fair, driven by fear rather than justice.

It was not until 1736 that Parliament passed an Act repealing the laws against witchcraft, marking an official end to the legal persecution of witches in England. However, the damage had already been done. Hundreds of lives were lost, and the terror of the witch hunts forever scarred countless more. The repeal itself was met with derision; when introduced in the House of Commons, the Bill caused laughter among MPs, a reflection of how the horrors of the past were already being forgotten. Even Sir Isaac Newton, a father of modern science, was deeply fascinated by the occult, demonstrating how intertwined these beliefs were with the fabric of society at the time.

The remnants of these laws lingered for centuries. The Vagrancy Act of 1824 made fortune-telling, astrology, and spiritualism punishable offences, while the Fraudulent Mediums Act, introduced in 1951, continued to regulate claims of supernatural powers until repealed in 2008.

This book is dedicated to the memory of all those women—mothers, daughters, sisters, and healers—who were persecuted under these draconian laws. Their lives were cut short by ignorance and fear, but their stories are a testament to the resilience of the human spirit in the face of unimaginable injustice. By telling their stories, we honour their memory and acknowledge the painful history that shaped the lives of so many.

Let this book serve as a reminder of the dangers of allowing fear to dictate justice and of the importance of safeguarding the rights and dignity of all people, regardless of the era or the circumstances. As we reflect on this history, may we also commit to ensuring that such tragedies are never repeated.

Chapter One: Morning in Blackthorn Hollow

The sun rose gently over Blackthorn Hollow, casting long shadows across the cobblestone streets. The village was a patchwork of timber-framed buildings with steeply pitched roofs and leaded windows, their wattle and daub walls blending soft, weathered whites and ochres. Each structure, from the smallest cottage to the largest manor, told stories of the generations who had lived there, their lives etched into the very beams that supported the walls.

The blacksmith's hammer rang out in the village square, a rhythmic beat that echoed through the narrow streets. The baker's shop filled the air with the scent of fresh bread, and the village children chased each other around the fountain, their laughter a brief respite from the worries that plagued the adults.

The Blackthorn sisters' house stood in a small cottage at the edge of the village, on a narrow lane winding its way through the centre. It was an ancient building, its wooden beams dark with age, twisted slightly as if the house had grown like a tree, adapting to the whims of time and weather. The house was slightly larger than the other cottages, its thatched roof sloping down toward the earth, giving it the appearance of a contented creature nestled into the landscape.

The windows of the house were small, with panes of glass held together by crisscrossing lead strips, distorting the light that entered. These windows were often the first sign to villagers that the sisters were awake and about their work. The Blackthorn sisters were known far and wide for their healing arts, their knowledge passed down through generations, and their home reflected the respect and fear with which they were regarded.

As the morning sun reached higher into the sky, a warm, golden light began to spill through the open windows of the sisters' home, revealing the collection of herbs hanging from the rafters to dry. Bundles of sage, rosemary, and lavender swayed gently in the breeze, their scents mingling to create a heady perfume that filled the air. On a sturdy wooden table near the hearth, jars filled with roots, dried flowers, and powders were neatly arranged, each labelled in Margaret Blackthorn's precise hand.

The village of Blackthorn Hollow was small; its residents were primarily farmers and craftsmen. The buildings clustered around the village square, dominated by the ancient church, its stone tower rising above the rooftops like a sentinel. The church, built in a time long forgotten, was a place of both worship and judgment. Here, Sir Edward Grantham, the local magistrate, held court, dispensing justice as he saw fit.

Sir Edward's manor house, located at the far end of the village, was a grand structure, its brickwork sharp and red against the muted tones of the village cottages. Unlike the other buildings, which seemed to merge seamlessly with the surrounding landscape, the manor was a symbol of power and authority, its large windows looking out over the village like the eyes of a watchful beast.

The people of Blackthorn Hollow had always relied on the sisters for their skills in times of need.

Eliza, the eldest of the Blackthorn sisters, was known throughout the village for her profound knowledge of herbs and their uses. The garden behind the house was a marvel—a vibrant tapestry of colours and scents. Carefully cultivated beds of chamomile, yarrow, and feverfew blossomed under her meticulous care. At the same time, the gnarled branches of elder and rowan trees stood heavy with berries and blossoms, offering their potent healing properties. This garden was not just a place of beauty but a sanctuary of remedies, each plant chosen with the precision of a seasoned healer.

Inside the house, Eliza stood by the hearth, her hands moving deftly through bundles of dried herbs. Her dark hair, streaked with silver, framed a face of striking sharpness—high cheekbones, a strong jawline, and deep brown eyes that held the quiet wisdom of years spent in service to others. Dressed in a simple, earth-toned dress, practical and worn, with an apron tied around her waist, stained from countless hours of work, she exuded a calm certainty that reassured those around her.

"Eliza, have you seen the hyssop?" Margaret's voice gently interrupted the morning's stillness. Her hazel eyes, soft and kind, searched the room with a hint of urgency.

Margaret, the middle sister with chestnut brown hair that fell in gentle waves around her shoulders, possessed a natural warmth that radiated a maternal aura. Dressed in a muted green gown, she embodied the calm and patience essential to the many births she had overseen. Her hands, steady and sure hands, brought most of the village's children into the world, and her soft and reassuring voice was a balm to those in distress. Yet, despite her indispensable role, the villagers were careful not to be seen seeking her advice, wary of the whispers of witchcraft that lingered like a shadow over the sisters.

Eliza looked up, a small, reassuring smile touching her lips. "I set it to dry near the hearth last night. It should be ready."

Anne, the youngest, was more reserved than her older sisters and her talents in preparing remedies and potions. Often found in the small room at the back of the house, her fingers moved with quiet intensity, grinding herbs and roots into fine powders or mixing tinctures and salves with the precision of an alchemist. Her focus was unnerving to those who did not know her well, and her silence was often mistaken for aloofness. Yet, within that silence was a deep well of knowledge, a quiet strength that matched the fervour of her work.

"You're a blessing to this village, Margaret," Anne said with a grin, her voice light. "I swear, you've saved more lives than anyone could count."

Margaret chuckled, the sound soft and melodious. "And you, Anne, could charm even the most stubborn patient into taking their medicine."

The sisters' mother, who had passed some years before, had taught them everything they knew. She had been a healer, too, and her reputation had extended far beyond the borders of Blackthorn Hollow. But with her death, the sisters had found themselves increasingly isolated, their work viewed with growing suspicion as fear of witchcraft spread across the land.

The sisters exchanged affectionate glances before returning to their tasks. Today, they were to gather foxglove, a rare and precious herb that grew in a hidden glen on their land. With its bell-shaped flowers, this plant held the key to treating heart ailments that had begun to trouble the village. It was not just any herb but essential for the lives of those who depended on their skills.

The sisters had always been close, their bond strengthened by their shared knowledge and the burdens they carried. They understood the power of their work, the delicate balance between healing and harm. They knew that the same herbs that could cure could also kill if misused. And they knew that the villagers, who depended on them in times of need, would not hesitate to turn on them if they believed it necessary.

As they stepped outside, the morning sunlight welcomed them, washing over the fields stretching around their cottage. The land was alive with colour, a patchwork of greens and purples dotted with the vibrant hues of the herbs they carefully cultivated. The world around them was peaceful, filled with the chirping of birds and the gentle rustling of leaves, a stark contrast to the rising fear and superstition in the world beyond Blackthorn Hollow.

THE PATH TO THE GLEN was narrow and winding, but the sisters knew it by heart. It was a sacred place where the earth seemed to pulse with life, and the trees whispered secrets to those who listened. Here, the sunlight filtered through the canopy in delicate beams, touching the ground with dappled light. The air was thick with the scent of rich soil and growing things, a reminder of their connection with the land.

Eliza moved with practised precision, her skilled hands carefully harvesting the foxglove. Margaret followed closely, her steady hands collecting the herbs with a reverence that spoke of her deep understanding of their power. Anne's swift and light movements worked alongside her sisters, her youthful energy contrasting with the ancient knowledge they wielded.

The sisters worked in silence, each lost in their thoughts. Yet, as they gathered the precious herb, a shadow passed over Eliza's heart. It was a fleeting sensation, a whisper of foreboding that she could not shake. She glanced at her sisters, wondering if they felt it too, but their faces were serene, untouched by the unease gnawing at her. Pushing the feeling aside, Eliza focused on the task at hand. There was much to do, and the villagers relied on them.

As they worked, the tranquillity of the glen seemed to embrace them, offering a temporary reprieve from the responsibilities that awaited them back in the village. For a brief moment, Eliza allowed herself to be fully present in this place, to feel the earth beneath her feet and the sunlight on her skin. It was a reminder of why they did what they did, of the deep connection they shared with the land and each other.

The morning air was still warm as the Blackthorn sisters returned to their cottage, baskets filled with the precious foxglove. The peace of Blackthorn

Hollow wrapped around them like a comforting cloak, yet Eliza couldn't shake the lingering sense of unease in her chest.

As they neared their home, the sight of a young man at their door broke the moment's serenity. He was frantic, his fist pounding against the wood, his shouts echoing across the quiet village.

"Please! You must come quickly!" he cried, desperation lacing his voice. "My mother—she needs help!"

The sisters quickened their pace, worry flashing across their faces. Eliza, her eyes narrowing with concern, reached the young man first. His face was pale, his hair dishevelled, and there was a wildness in his eyes that spoke of fear.

"What's happened?" Eliza asked, her voice steady despite the urgency in her heart.

"It's my mother," he gasped, barely catching his breath. "She's in terrible pain. We don't know what to do—please, you have to help her!"

Margaret stepped forward, her hands reaching out to steady the young man. Her hazel eyes, usually so calm, were now sharp with focus. "Is it her time? Has she been ill?"

The young man shook his head, trembling. "She's been healthy, but now... now she can't breathe, and she's clutching her chest. Please, come quickly!"

Eliza exchanged a brief glance with Margaret and Anne. Without another word, they moved into action, their previous task forgotten as they gathered their supplies. Anne, her youthful energy now directed with purpose, grabbed their satchels, already packed with herbs and tinctures. Margaret retrieved the foxglove they had just harvested, its potent properties possibly needed for the woman's heart.

"Lead the way," Eliza instructed, her voice firm and authoritative.

The young man nodded, relief washing over his features as he turned and began running back the way he had come. The sisters followed close behind, their skirts rustling through the tall grass as they hurried to the aid of yet another villager.

As they ran, Eliza couldn't help but feel the weight of her earlier premonition pressing down on her. She pushed the thought aside, focusing on the path ahead. Now was not the time for fear; now was the time for action. But deep down, she knew that this was only the beginning.

The sisters followed the young man through the winding streets of Blackthorn Hollow, their pace swift and determined. Usually so calm and picturesque, the village seemed to blur around them as they hurried. The sense of urgency pressed in on them, their thoughts focused entirely on the woman who awaited their help.

The young man led them to a small, dilapidated cottage that stood alone, its isolation contrasting with the close-knit homes they had passed earlier. The roof sagged under the weight of age, the thatch worn thin in places, threatening to give way entirely. The wooden walls, once sturdy, were now weathered and cracked, marked by the passage of many harsh winters. The entire structure leaned slightly as though tired from years of holding itself up.

Without hesitation, the young man pushed open the creaking door, leading the sisters inside. The air within the cottage was thick and heavy, carrying the musty scent of damp wood and stale air. The dim light from the windows barely penetrated the shadows that clung to the corners of the small, cluttered room.

The sisters' eyes quickly found the woman they had come to help. She lay on the floor in front of the hearth, her body curled in on itself as if trying to contain the pain wracking her frame. Her hair, once a rich dark brown, was now streaked with grey, and her face, though lined with age, bore the unmistakable signs of suffering. Her hands clutched her chest, and her breath came in short, ragged gasps. Tears streamed down her cheeks, her sobs punctuating the eerie silence of the room.

"Mother!" the young man cried as he knelt beside her, his voice trembling with fear. He looked up at the sisters, his eyes pleading. "Please, help her!"

Eliza knelt beside the woman, her face a mask of calm determination. She gently touched the woman's forehead, feeling the cold sweat that clung to her skin. "Shh, it's all right. We're here now," she whispered soothingly. Her deep brown eyes flicked to Margaret and Anne, who immediately moved into action.

With her steady hands, Margaret began to unpack the satchels, laying out the herbs and tinctures they had brought. "Her pulse is weak," she murmured, her voice laced with concern as she took the woman's hand, feeling the faint, erratic rhythm of her heartbeat. "It could be her heart."

Her youthful energy now focused and deliberate, Anne quickly crushed the fresh foxglove they had gathered, mixing it with water to prepare a tincture.

Her green eyes were bright with concentration as she worked, her movements swift and efficient.

"We need to get this into her quickly," Anne said, her voice steady. "Foxglove can help strengthen her heart, but we must be careful with the dosage."

Eliza nodded, her gaze returning to the woman, who was now looking up at her with wide, terrified eyes. "Can you hear me?" Eliza asked gently, her voice firm but compassionate. The woman nodded weakly, tears still streaming down her face. "We'll give you something to help your heart, but you need to trust us, right?"

The woman managed a small, shaky nod. Eliza helped her sit up slightly, supporting her as Margaret held the cup to her lips. "Sip slowly," Margaret instructed, her tone calm and soothing. The woman obeyed, taking small, careful sips of the tincture.

As the minutes passed, the sisters watched anxiously for any improvement. The tension in the room was palpable, the young man's eyes darting between his mother and the sisters, his fear evident in every nervous twitch.

Gradually, the woman's breathing began to steady, the harsh, ragged gasps giving way to slower, more even breaths. Her grip on her chest loosened, and the tight lines of pain etched into her face began to soften. The tincture was working.

Margaret exchanged a relieved glance with Eliza, who nodded in acknowledgement. "You're going to be all right," Eliza assured the woman, now lying back with a weary but calmer expression. "But you must rest. Your heart has been through a great strain."

The young man let out a breath he hadn't realised he was holding, his shoulders sagging with relief. "Thank you... thank you so much," he whispered, his voice choked with emotion.

Eliza gave him a reassuring smile, though her mind was already turning to the next steps. "She'll need to take it easy for a while," she advised. "No sudden movements or exertions. We'll leave you with more tincture and return to check on her in the morning."

Anne, ever practical, began to tidy up the remnants of their work while Margaret carefully measured out more doses of the foxglove tincture. The sisters moved with the ease and precision of those who had done this many times before, their years of experience evident in every motion.

As they prepared to leave, Eliza glanced around the small cottage. The sense of unease from earlier had not entirely dissipated. The cottage, with its worn walls and neglected garden, seemed to carry a weight of sorrow as if the struggles of its occupants had seeped into the very wood and stone.

She turned to the young man, kneeling beside his mother, holding her hand as she drifted into a fitful sleep. "Take care of her," Eliza said softly. "And if anything changes, send for us immediately."

He nodded, his eyes filled with gratitude. "I will. I promise."

With their work done, the sisters quietly left the dilapidated cottage, stepping out into the daylight. The sun was still shining, but it seemed warmer, brighter than before, as if in stark contrast to the gloom they had just left behind. However, the air was heavy, almost oppressive, as if the world held its breath.

As they returned home, a sense of unease settled over Eliza. The peace of Blackthorn Hollow, once so comforting, now felt fragile, as though it could shatter at the slightest disturbance. The memory of the woman's stricken face lingered in her mind, a reminder that even in their secluded village, darkness could find its way in.

Eliza glanced up at the sky, her thoughts troubled, and noticed a change. The bright blue expanse had begun to dim, the sunlight fading as dark clouds gathered on the horizon. They moved swiftly, rolling in like a tide, blotting out the sun and casting long shadows over the land. The sudden shift was unsettling, as if the very air was charged with a warning.

"We should hurry," Margaret said, her hazel eyes lifting to the sky as well, her voice tight with concern. "There's a storm coming."

Anne, always quick to react, pulled her shawl tighter around her shoulders, her green eyes flickering with a mix of excitement and apprehension. "Let's go, then," she urged, her voice carrying an edge of urgency.

As the sisters quickened their pace, the first flash of lightning split the sky, followed by the ominous rumble of thunder that seemed to shake the earth beneath their feet. The storm was upon them with startling speed as if an unseen force drew it. The wind picked up, whipping their hair around their faces and tugging at their skirts.

Then, the heavens opened. Rain poured down in torrents, drenching them in an instant. The sisters lifted their skirts and began to run, their feet splashing through the quickly forming puddles as they raced along the muddy path back to their cottage.

The storm was fierce, the wind howling through the trees, bending their branches low. The once familiar path became treacherous underfoot, the rain turning the earth into slick mud that threatened to pull them down with every step. But the sisters pressed on, their breaths gasping as they struggled against the elements.

Eliza led the way, her heart pounding from the exertion and a growing sense of dread that gnawed at the edges of her thoughts. The storm felt unnatural, its sudden ferocity mirroring the shadow of unease that had been stalking her since that morning.

At last, their cottage came into view, a small beacon of warmth and safety amid the storm's chaos. They stumbled through the doorway, breathless and soaked to the bone, slamming the door against the fury outside. The sound of the rain beating against the thatch roof was deafening, the wind howling like a wild beast.

They stood for a moment in the dim light of their cottage, water pooling at their feet as they caught their breath. Anne laughed nervously, pushing her wet hair out of her face. "Well, that was something, wasn't it?"

But neither Eliza nor Margaret shared in her attempt at lightness. Eliza's mind was racing, the day's events spinning in her thoughts. She moved to the window, peering out into the storm, her gaze searching the darkened sky.

"It came on so suddenly," Margaret murmured, wringing out her sodden skirts. "Like it was waiting for us."

Eliza said nothing, her eyes fixed on the horizon where the storm clouds churned like a living thing. The peace of Blackthorn Hollow had been shattered, and with it, the sense of safety that had always been their refuge.

She turned back to her sisters, her expression grim. "This is only the beginning," she said quietly, her voice barely audible over the storm's roar.

"Something is coming, and I fear it's darker than we can imagine."

The words hung in the air, heavy with the weight of prophecy. Outside, the storm raged on, its fury a harbinger of trials yet to come.

Chapter Two: The Historian's Calling

Dr. Emily Ward sat at her mahogany desk, the late afternoon sun casting a warm glow across her office. Outside, light snow had begun to fall, blanketing the university grounds in a pristine layer of white. The winter chill seeped through the old windows, but inside, Emily's office was a haven of warmth and history. The room was a sanctuary for the historian, filled with shelves upon shelves of old books, documents, and artefacts—each one a silent witness to the dark and often misunderstood history she had dedicated her life to studying. The scent of aged paper and leather-bound volumes lingered in the air, a comforting reminder of the centuries of knowledge within these walls.

Emily's office, tucked away in a quiet corner of the university where she worked, was more than just a place of research. It was a repository for the past, a curated collection of evidence from witchcraft trials across Europe. Each item held a story—some tragic, some mysterious—all bound by the common thread of fear and persecution. Her desk was cluttered with notes, sketches, and old court records, all carefully organised to aid her in piecing together the fragmented history of the women and men who had been accused of witchcraft.

With her sharp intellect and unyielding curiosity, Emily had become one of her field's foremost historians. Her research focused not just on the events of the witch trials themselves but on the lives of the accused—the healers, midwives, and wise women who had been systematically silenced by the societies that once relied on their knowledge. She had spent countless hours delving into the lives of these women, seeking to understand who they were beyond the accusations that had led to their persecution.

Today, Emily was deep into her research on the witch trials of Pendelford, a village in the north of England known for one of the most notorious cases in the 17th century. Her desk was cluttered with notes, sketches, and court records—pieces of a puzzle she had spent years trying to assemble. The women and men accused in Pendelford had suffered greatly, their lives torn apart by fear and superstition, and Emily was determined to uncover every detail of their stories.

With her mind already racing ahead to the work that awaited her in Blackthorn Hollow, Emily turned off the lamp on her desk, casting the room into shadows. She paused momentarily, her hand resting on the doorframe as she looked back at the collection of history she had curated. This was where her journey had begun, but she knew it was far from over.

She leaned closer to a particularly old document, her sharp blue eyes scanning the faded text. Her auburn hair fell loosely over her shoulders as she read, her focus intense. She was in her element, completely absorbed in the work that had defined her career as a historian and curator of evidence from witchcraft trials. The mysteries of the past were her passion, and each new discovery brought her closer to understanding the lives of those persecuted.

A soft knock on the door broke her concentration. Emily looked up, slightly startled, as the door creaked open to reveal her colleague, Professor Robert Avery. He was a tall, slightly stooped man in his late fifties with greying hair and a kind smile that always seemed to hold a secret. He held a worn leather folder in his hands, its edges frayed from years of use.

"Emily, I hope I'm not interrupting," Robert said, stepping into the room. "But I found something in the archives that I thought you might find interesting."

Emily sat back in her chair, her curiosity piqued. "Not at all, Robert. What have you got there?"

Robert crossed the room and placed the folder on her desk, his eyes twinkling with the excitement of discovery. "I know you've been focused on the Pendelford trials, but I found something in our southern archives that might divert your attention—at least for a little while. It's from a small village in Essex called Blackthorn Hollow."

Emily raised an eyebrow as she reached for the folder. "Blackthorn Hollow? I don't believe I've come across that name before."

"It's not well-known," Robert admitted, sitting across from her. "The village is still inhabited, but its history is rather obscure. I stumbled upon these documents while looking into something else. I thought of you immediately."

Emily opened the folder, her fingers brushing over the rough edges of the old paper. Inside, she found several hand-drawn sketches, faded and yellowed with age, depicting a trio of women. Their faces were solemn, their eyes staring out from the page with an intensity that sent a chill down her spine. Beneath the drawings were pages of handwritten notes, trial records, and what appeared to be excerpts from personal letters.

"These drawings... who are they?" Emily asked, her voice barely above a whisper as she carefully examined the delicate paper.

"They were ordinary women," Robert explained, "but their names—Eliza, Margaret, and Anne—have been preserved in whispers and fragments of history. They were accused of witchcraft in the late 16th century, during the height of the Essex witch trials. Like many others, their story is tragic, but something about their case differs. The records are unusually scarce, almost as if they were deliberately erased. The trial was overshadowed by larger events, yet the village they lived in has been haunted by strange occurrences ever since. Some say it all traces back to them."

"Why hasn't this come up before?" Emily asked, her eyes flicking back to the drawings, captivated by the haunted expressions of the sisters.

"That's part of what makes it so intriguing," Robert replied, leaning forward. "The village has done a good job keeping its secrets. The few existing records were scattered across various collections, and it wasn't until I stumbled upon this folder that the pieces started coming together. I thought you might want to take a look."

Emily nodded slowly, her mind already racing with possibilities. The Pendelford trials were important, but this—this felt like the beginning of something even more significant.

"Thank you, Robert," she said, her voice filled with genuine appreciation. "This could be exactly what I've been looking for. I think it's time I took a trip south."

Robert smiled, pleased to have sparked her interest. "I thought you might say that. Just be careful, Emily. Blackthorn Hollow is still a small, close-knit community. Not everyone there will be eager to talk about the past."

Emily nodded, already planning her next steps. "I'll be cautious. But if there's one thing I've learned, the truth has a way of revealing itself—no matter how deeply it's buried."

With that, Robert took his leave, and Emily returned her focus to the folder before her. As she carefully studied the documents, a sense of excitement and foreboding filled her.

The winter sky had darkened by the time Dr. Emily Ward left the university, the snow still falling softly around her as she made her way to the parking lot. Her mind was abuzz with thoughts of Blackthorn Hollow, the mysterious village in Essex that had suddenly become the focal point of her research. The folder Robert had given her was tucked securely under her arm, and she couldn't wait to dive deeper into its contents.

Emily's drive home was peaceful, the roads nearly empty as the snow blanketed the world in a quiet, serene white. Her apartment was a modern contrast to the ancient history she spent her days studying. Located just outside the town centre, it was spacious and filled with natural light, with large windows that now framed a wintry scene of softly falling snow. The clean lines and minimalist decor were softened by warm textiles and the soft glow of well-placed lamps, making it a cosy retreat.

As she stepped inside, the warmth of the apartment embraced her, the quiet only broken by the occasional crackle from the fireplace, which had been set up by her partner before he left for work. Emily's gaze fell on a note on the kitchen counter, written in his familiar, hurried scrawl: *"Called into the hospital—don't wait up. See you tomorrow. Love, James."*

She smiled faintly, her fingers brushing over the note before she set it aside. James was a doctor, often called into work at odd hours. It was a part of his life she had grown accustomed to, though she missed his presence during the quiet evenings they shared. Tonight, however, she had something else to occupy her thoughts.

After shedding her boots and coat, Emily poured herself a glass of red wine and carried it into the living room. The apartment was quiet; the only sound was the occasional crackle from the fireplace that James had prepared for her. She set the folder on the coffee table, then curled up on the sofa, her legs tucked beneath her as she took a sip of the wine, savouring its warmth.

With a deep breath, Emily opened the folder and began to sift through the documents again, her fingers brushing over the faded sketches and handwritten notes. The three women—Eliza, Margaret, and Anne—seemed to watch her from across the centuries, their solemn faces rendered in delicate, time-worn lines. As she studied the drawings, fragments of their lives began to shape her mind. They were ordinary women thrust into extraordinary circumstances during the hysteria of the witch hunts that had swept across England. As captured in the sketches, their faces bore haunting and defiant expressions, as if they were silently challenging the world that had condemned them.

One document, in particular, caught her attention. It was an old, faded drawing that appeared to be some sort of map. The paper was brittle, the ink blurred in places, and the details were difficult to make out. Emily held it closer, squinting at the faint lines and shapes. It was clearly a map of some kind, but its meaning was obscured by time. Small symbols dotted the page, possibly indicating landmarks or buildings, but they were indistinct, almost ghostly.

She stared at the map for a long moment, trying to decipher it. The lines seemed familiar, yet nothing on the map immediately stood out. The more she looked, the more it intrigued her, the mystery of it pulling her deeper into thought. Almost unconsciously, she leaned forward, her breath catching as she whispered to herself, "What is your story?"

Soft and low, the question hung in the air as if she were addressing the centuries-old document itself. What was this map trying to tell her? What secrets did it hold about Blackthorn Hollow and the women who had lived there so long ago?

Emily squinted at the drawing, trying to discern its meaning. The lines and shapes were faint, but they suggested the outline of a landscape, with markings that could be roads or pathways. Small symbols were scattered across the page—perhaps indicating landmarks or buildings—but their meaning was unclear. It looked like a map, but to what?

Setting her wine down, Emily reached for her laptop. She needed to know more. As the screen flickered to life, she typed "Blackthorn Hollow Essex" into the search engine, her fingers moving quickly over the keys. She found a few references to the village—a small, still-inhabited place in the south of England—but nothing that seemed to explain the map in front of her.

She pulled up an image of the village from an old map she found in a digital archive, her eyes darting between the screen and the faded drawing. The modern map showed the current layout of Blackthorn Hollow—its narrow roads, the village square, and the surrounding countryside. But the old drawing in front of her was different, older, with details that didn't quite match the present-day layout.

Emily zoomed in on the map, tracing the roads with her finger, trying to align them with the faint lines on the ancient document. There was something familiar about the drawing, but the passage of time had blurred its details, making it difficult to pinpoint exactly what it depicted. Still, she couldn't shake the feeling that this map—whatever it was—held the key to understanding the Blackthorn sisters' story.

After several minutes of careful comparison, she noticed a small symbol on the modern map and the old drawing—a cross, likely indicating a church. It was one of the few points that seemed to match the two maps, giving her a starting point. The cross on the old map was positioned near what looked like a cluster of buildings, possibly a village or settlement. Could this be an older version of Blackthorn Hollow?

Emily's heart raced as she continued her search, now looking for historical references that might link Blackthorn Hollow to the mysterious map. She found a few old records that mentioned the village but needed to be more sparse and provide more context. Still, the pieces were beginning to come together.

The map might be a key—an ancient guide to a version of Blackthorn Hollow that had long since changed or perhaps even been forgotten. The question was, what was it meant to reveal? And why had it been hidden among the documents of a forgotten witch trial?

As she stared at the faded lines of the drawing, Emily felt a thrill of anticipation. She was on the verge of uncovering something significant that had been buried for centuries.

With her laptop open and the map before her, she spent the rest of the evening immersed in research, following every lead and clue that might help her decipher the mysterious drawing. The wine sat forgotten on the table as Emily became lost in the past, driven by the need to uncover the truth.

It was 4 a.m. when Emily was gently awoken by the touch of a hand on her shoulder. Blinking groggily, she looked up to see James standing over her, his face softened by the dim light from the hallway. The fire in the fireplace had long since burned out, leaving the room chilly and dark. The only light came from the soft glow of her laptop screen, still open on the coffee table where she had been working.

"Emily," James whispered, concern lacing his voice. "You fell asleep at your laptop again."

Emily sat up slowly, rubbing her eyes as the events of the evening came rushing back. The folder from Robert, the mysterious map, and her feverish search for answers had consumed her until she'd finally succumbed to exhaustion. The wine glass was still half full on the table, forgotten as she'd buried herself in her work.

"I must have dozed off," she murmured, glancing at the screen, which now displayed a half-completed search for historical records on Blackthorn Hollow. The map she had been studying was still laid before her, its faded lines barely visible in the dim light.

James glanced at the papers scattered across the table, his brow furrowing slightly as he took in the faded map and old documents. He was used to Emily's late-night research sessions and her relentless pursuit of historical truths. However, seeing her asleep at her laptop, surrounded by ancient artefacts, always concerned him. He hated seeing her push herself to exhaustion.

James knelt beside her, his presence warm and reassuring. He gently closed her laptop and moved it aside, his fingers brushing hers. "You need to take care of yourself, Em. You can't keep working like this."

"I know," Emily sighed, leaning into him as he wrapped an arm around her. "I just... I found something, James. Something important, I think. It's an old map. I've been trying to figure out what it means."

James gave her a gentle smile, his eyes filled with warmth. "You'll figure it out; you always do. But not tonight. You need to get some rest."

Emily nodded, the adrenaline from earlier fading as the reality of the late hour settled in. She knew he was right—she was no good to her research if she was too tired to think straight. "I suppose you're right," she admitted, stifling a yawn. "I didn't mean to fall asleep out here."

James helped her to her feet, guiding her away from the sofa and towards their bedroom. "Come on, let's get you to bed. We can deal with this in the morning."

As they walked through the darkened apartment, Emily couldn't help but cast one last glance at the map on the coffee table. The mystery of Blackthorn

Hollow still tugged at her thoughts, but for now, she let herself lean into the comfort of James's presence, grateful for his steady support.

The room was quiet as they settled into bed, the weight of the day and the night finally catching up with her. As she drifted off to sleep, Emily's mind replayed the question she had asked herself earlier, her voice a whisper in the stillness: *What is your story?*

The answer would come; she was sure of it. But for now, she allowed herself to rest, knowing that she would return to the search in the morning with renewed focus.

Chapter Three: The Sisters Craft

The warm glow of the hearth filled the small kitchen with a comforting light as the Blackthorn sisters gathered around the heavy wooden table, their hands busy with the tasks of their craft. The scent of fresh herbs hung in the air, mingling with the earthy aroma of the firewood crackling in the hearth. The room was cosy, its walls lined with shelves full of dried plants, jars of tinctures, and carefully bound scrolls of handwritten notes passed down through generations.

Eliza sat at the head of the table, her long, dark hair pulled back from her face as she carefully ground a mixture of comfrey and yarrow in a stone mortar. Her hands moved with practised ease, the muscles in her forearms flexing as she worked. Her deep brown eyes were focused, every movement precise as she prepared a salve for wounds—one that would soon be needed by a villager who had taken a nasty fall.

"That should do it," Eliza murmured to herself, satisfied with the consistency of the paste. She set the mortar aside and carefully reached for a small glass jar, spooning the mixture into it. The salve would need to be ready by the time the villager arrived, his injury already known to the sisters by the swift messages that always seemed to reach them before any other aid could.

Across from her, Margaret was busy preparing a different concoction. Her hands, steady and sure, worked swiftly as she blended raspberry leaf with nettle and chamomile, a soothing tea for a woman who was about to give birth. Margaret's hazel eyes, warm and kind, were filled with concentration as she worked, her mind focused on the mother-to-be who would soon need her help.

"The Vaughans' child will be here by morning, I suspect," Margaret said quietly, her voice carrying the calm confidence from years of midwifery. She set the mixture aside, ready to be brewed when the time came.

Anne, the youngest, sat near the window, her auburn hair catching the firelight as she carefully tied bundles of lavender and rosemary with twine.

Her green eyes sparkled with youthful energy, though her movements were as skilled and deliberate as her sisters'. She was preparing the herbs to hang above the birthing bed, their scent calming the labouring mother and cleansing the air.

"The wind has picked up," Anne remarked, glancing out the window where the branches of the nearby trees swayed in the evening breeze. "The night will be cold, but the tea and herbs should keep her warm and comfortable."

Eliza nodded, her gaze still on the salve she was sealing with a waxed cloth. "We must be prepared for anything," she said, her tone serious. "Childbirth is never without risk, but we'll do everything we can to ensure a safe delivery."

The sisters continued their work in a comfortable silence. Each focused on their tasks yet aware of the other's presence, their bond evident in how they moved together. Their kitchen, filled with the tools and scents of their trade, was a place of warmth and purpose, a sanctuary where they practised the healing arts passed down through their family for generations.

Outside, the night deepened, the wind whispering through the trees as if carrying secrets on its breath. The village of Blackthorn Hollow was quiet, its inhabitants settling in for the evening, unaware of the quiet preparations taking place in the Blackthorn cottage. All was calm for now, but the sisters knew their work was never done. The village depended on them, and they were ready to answer the call, as they always had.

The Blackthorn sisters finished their preparations as the night deepened, the kitchen's warmth and the hearth's glow creating a cocoon of comfort around them. With the salves and teas ready and the herbs neatly bundled, they began to unwind, the day's work slowly giving way to the quiet rituals of the evening.

Eliza was the first to rise from the table, and her work was complete for the night. She moved to the stove, where a pot of stew had been simmering, filling the room with its rich, savoury aroma. The stew had been bubbling gently for hours, a comforting blend of root vegetables, lentils, and herbs they had grown in their garden. She ladled the thick stew into three wooden bowls, the meal's warmth promising to ward off the evening chill. The sisters gathered around the table again, sharing a meal that brought peace after the day's labours.

They ate in companionable silence, the clink of spoons against the bowls the only sound in the room. The stew was hearty, with the earthy sweetness of parsnips and the peppery bite of fresh thyme. As they ate, the warmth of the meal spread through them, easing the tension of the day. Though often immersed in their work, the sisters found comfort in these quiet moments together, where the burdens of their roles as healers could be momentarily set aside.

Margaret paused, looking at her sisters with a small, contented smile. "This reminds me of the first winter we spent here after Mother passed," she said softly, her voice tinged with nostalgia. "We were so young then, trying to carry on her work."

Eliza nodded, her expression thoughtful as she remembered those early days. "We had so much to learn. But she taught us well."

Ever the optimist, Anne grinned as she wiped her bowl clean with a piece of crusty bread. "And look at us now. The whole village relies on us. Mother would be proud."

As they finished their meal, Margaret rose to clear the table, her movements efficient yet unhurried. Always full of energy, Anne hopped up to help, carrying the bowls to the sink, where she began washing them with water heated on the stove. The rhythmic splash of water and the quiet hum of the night created a soothing background as they tidied up, their actions part of a well-worn routine.

Eliza, content after the meal, stoked the fire one last time before setting a kettle to boil. The sisters often ended their evenings with herbal tea, a tradition that calmed their minds and prepared them for sleep. Tonight, Eliza chose a blend of chamomile, lemon balm, and a hint of valerian—herbs known for their calming properties. She prepared the tea with practised ease, the steam rising from the pot in fragrant tendrils.

Eliza took a moment to check the kitchen shelves as the tea brewed, her fingers brushing over the carefully labelled jars of herbs and remedies. She mentally noted what would need replenishing soon—especially the winter stocks of elderberry syrup and thyme, essential for keeping colds and fevers at bay during the colder months.

Once the tea was ready, the sisters gathered in the small sitting area near the hearth, their steaming mugs cradled in their hands. The fire crackled softly, casting dancing shadows across the walls as they sipped their tea, the warmth of the drink easing the tensions of the day.

"This is just what we needed," Margaret murmured, her hazel eyes half-closed as she savoured the tea's soothing effects. The gentle blend of herbs relaxed her, easing the tightness in her shoulders that had built up from a long day of work.

Anne nodded, her usually bright green eyes now softened by the dim light and the calming herbs. "It's been a busy day, but I could sleep for a week after this."

Eliza smiled faintly, her thoughts drifting toward the rest that awaited them. "We'll need our strength. The Vaughans will call for us soon, and the night might be long."

They finished their tea in peaceful silence, the comforting routine a balm for their weary souls. Once the mugs were set aside, the sisters moved through the small cottage, preparing for bed. The tasks were simple—extinguishing the lamps, checking that the herbs were stored properly, and ensuring that everything was in its place should they be called upon in the middle of the night.

Finally, they went to their shared bedroom, a cosy space with three small beds covered in hand-stitched quilts. The room was simple but warm, with dried herbs hanging from the rafters and a single candle flickering on the nightstand. The sisters changed into their nightclothes, the fabric soft against their skin, worn from years of use.

As they settled into their beds, the room fell into a comfortable silence, the only sound the distant howl of the wind outside. Eliza, lying on her back, stared up at the ceiling, her mind already drifting to thoughts of the day ahead. Would the birth go smoothly? Would the remedies they had prepared be enough? These questions were familiar, a constant undercurrent in her thoughts, but she took comfort in knowing they had done everything they could to be ready.

Margaret, always the nurturer, turned on her side, breathing deep and steady, a sign that she was already asleep. She felt a quiet satisfaction in knowing she had helped another mother prepare for the arrival of new life, a task that never lost its significance no matter how many times she had done it.

Anne, still brimming with a hint of energy, snuggled under her quilt, a contented sigh escaping her lips. She enjoyed these moments just before sleep when the world seemed to hold its breath, and all was quiet and still. Her thoughts were light, flitting from one pleasant memory to another until she, too, felt the pull of sleep.

The candle's light flickered and dimmed as the sisters gradually succumbed to rest, their minds and bodies finally at peace. Outside, Blackthorn Hollow lay quiet, the villagers unaware of the unseen forces that shaped their lives. But within the Blackthorn cottage, the sisters slept soundly, knowing they were prepared for the night or the days to come.

The early morning light barely filtered through the thick canopy of trees surrounding Blackthorn Hollow, casting a pale greyness over the village. The night had passed peacefully, with the wind dying to a soft whisper, but as the first hints of dawn crept into the sky, the tranquillity was abruptly shattered.

A loud banging echoed through the Blackthorn cottage, the sound urgent and unrelenting. The front door rattled on its hinges as someone outside pounded on it, accompanied by shouts that pierced the early morning silence.

"Hello! Hello! Is there anyone there?"

The sisters awoke with a start, their hearts pounding as they scrambled out of bed. The urgency in the voice outside left no doubt—something was wrong. Eliza was the first to move, her instincts kicking in as she grabbed her shawl and hurried toward the door. Margaret and Anne were close behind, their minds racing as they quickly prepared for whatever awaited them.

Eliza reached the door and pulled it open, revealing a young man standing on the doorstep, his breath coming in harsh gasps, his face pale and streaked with sweat. He was clearly distraught, his eyes wide with fear and desperation.

"Please," he begged, his voice hoarse from shouting. "You must come quickly. It's my wife—something's gone wrong with the birth!"

Margaret stepped forward, her hands steady as she placed them on the young man's shoulders, trying to calm him. "Take a deep breath and tell us what's happened."

The man nodded, his breaths coming in quick, shallow bursts as he tried to explain. "She—she was in labour all night. But now—now she's bleeding, and the baby hasn't come. She's in so much pain—I don't know what to do!"

Margaret's eyes met Eliza's in a flash of understanding. They had seen this before, and they knew the situation was dire. Anne was already moving, gathering the necessary supplies into a satchel.

"We'll come right away," Eliza assured the man, her voice calm and authoritative. "Lead the way."

The young man wasted no time, turning on his heel and running back toward the path that led to his home, his footsteps heavy with fear and urgency. The sisters followed closely behind, their hearts pounding as they hurried to reach the needy woman. The cold morning air bit at their skin, the ground still damp from the night's dew, but they barely noticed, their minds focused entirely on the task ahead.

As they made their way through the village, the usually quiet streets were eerily empty, the villagers still tucked away in their homes, unaware of the life-or-death struggle just a few doors down. The sisters' footsteps echoed in the stillness, the situation's urgency lending them speed and purpose.

When they reached the young man's cottage, the door was already open, and they rushed inside without hesitation. The scene that greeted them was one of chaos and fear. The room was dimly lit by a single flickering candle, casting long shadows across the small space. In the corner, a woman lay on a makeshift bed, her face contorted in pain, her breathing laboured and uneven. The sheets beneath her were stained with blood, the sight of it stark and alarming in the dim light.

Margaret immediately went to the woman's side, her eyes scanning the situation with the calm focus of someone who had seen this before. She knelt beside the bed, gently touching the woman's forehead. The skin was clammy and cool, a sign of shock.

Stay with me," Margaret said softly, her voice a soothing balm in the tense atmosphere. "We're here now. We'll take care of you."

Eliza was already at work, setting out the herbs and tinctures they had brought. "Anne, prepare the motherwort and shepherd's purse," she instructed, her voice steady. "We need to stop the bleeding."

Anne moved quickly, her hands a blur as she mixed the herbs into a strong tea, the steam rising in fragrant tendrils. Her usually bright energy was now channelled into swift efficiency, every movement precise and purposeful.

Margaret checked the woman's pulse, feeling the faint, rapid flutter beneath her fingers. "She's weak, but she's holding on. We need to work quickly."

Eliza nodded, her eyes narrowing as she prepared a poultice to help with the pain. "We'll get through this. We have to."

The young man hovered near the bed, his eyes wide with fear as he watched the sisters work. He looked to Eliza, his voice trembling. "Is she going to be all right? Please—you have to save her."

Eliza looked up, her expression firm but kind. "We're doing everything we can. Your wife is strong, and so are we. But you must trust us and stay calm for her sake."

He nodded, swallowing hard as he took a step back, his hands wringing together in helpless anxiety.

The sisters worked silently, their actions coordinated and sure as they fought to save mother and child. The room was thick with the scent of herbs and the tension of the moment, every second stretching into what felt like an eternity.

Finally, after what seemed like hours but was likely only minutes, the bleeding began to slow, and the woman's breathing steadied, her face relaxing slightly as the pain started to ease. Margaret kept a close watch on her, whispering words of encouragement and comfort as Eliza and Anne continued their work, preparing for the final stages of the birth.

The baby, still not born, was now the focus of their attention. Margaret positioned herself to assist with the delivery, her hands gentle yet firm as she guided the mother through the most critical moments.

"One more push," Margaret urged her voice a mixture of strength and reassurance. "You're almost there."

The young woman, exhausted and terrified, summoned the last of her strength, and with a final, desperate effort, the baby came into the world. The room was momentarily still, the tension so thick it could be cut with a knife, as everyone held their breath.

Then, a tiny cry broke the silence.

Relief flooded the room as the baby's wail filled the air. Margaret quickly cleaned and wrapped the newborn, her hands trembling slightly with the release of tension. She handed the baby to the mother, who, though weak, managed a tearful smile as she cradled her child.

"You did it," Margaret whispered, her voice filled with emotion. "You're both safe now."

The young man, who had been standing frozen near the doorway, rushed to his wife's side, tears streaming down his face as he looked at their newborn child. "Thank you," he choked out, his voice thick with gratitude. "Thank you so much."

Eliza and Anne shared a look of quiet satisfaction as they began to clean up, the adrenaline of the moment starting to fade. They had done what they came to do, and once again, they had helped bring new life into the world.

As the sisters prepared to leave, Margaret gave the young mother one last piece of advice. "Rest now, and let your body recover. We'll come back to check on you later today. You're strong—you'll be just fine."

The woman nodded, her eyes heavy with exhaustion but filled with a deep sense of relief. She held her baby close, her grip protective and full of love.

The sisters stepped out of the cottage into the cold morning air, the first light of dawn just beginning to touch the horizon. The village was still quiet, the morning events unknown to all but those within the cottage.

Eliza breathed in the crisp air, feeling the weight of the night lift from her shoulders. "Another life saved," she murmured, a small smile tugging at her lips.

Margaret nodded, her hazel eyes bright with the satisfaction of a well-done job. "And a new one began."

Anne, though tired, was already looking forward. "We should get some rest ourselves. But first, maybe another cup of that tea?"

The sisters laughed softly, their bond stronger than ever as they returned to their cottage. The village was stirring now, the day beginning in earnest. But for the Blackthorn sisters, their work was already done—at least for now. They would rest, recharge, and be ready for whatever came next, knowing that the people of Blackthorn Hollow would always need them, and they would always be there to answer the call.

Chapter Four: The Journey to Blackthorn Hollow

The morning light streamed through the kitchen window, casting a warm glow across the sleek surfaces of Emily's modern apartment. She sat at the breakfast bar, a steaming cup of coffee in hand, her laptop open before her. Her thoughts were consumed by the mystery of Blackthorn Hollow, the small village in Essex that had suddenly become the focus of her research. The folder Robert had given her lay beside the laptop, its contents still fresh in her mind.

Emily had spent most of the night thinking about the village and the strange events that seemed tied to its history. As she prepared for her journey, she searched for a place to stay during her visit. The idea of staying in a quaint cottage appealed to her—something with character and history, a place that would immerse her in the atmosphere of the village.

James had wanted to come with her. He had been intrigued by the mysterious village, sharing in her excitement over the possibility of uncovering something significant. But his responsibilities at the hospital had kept him busy, and he reluctantly agreed to join her later in the week once his schedule allowed. They had shared a long conversation over breakfast the day before, discussing the trip and the possibility of him joining her, but ultimately, his work had to come first. "I'll be there as soon as I can," he had promised, his voice warm and reassuring.

She scrolled through listings on a travel website, her eyes skimming over various options. Most were small bed-and-breakfasts or modern accommodations, but they all felt entirely wrong. She was about to give up and settle for a standard inn when a particular listing caught her eye: "Charming Cottage in Blackthorn Hollow—Perfect for a Quiet Retreat."

The listing featured a single image of an old stone cottage nestled among trees, its thatched roof and ivy-covered walls giving it a timeless, almost enchanted appearance. The description was brief but intriguing, mentioning that the cottage had been recently restored and was available for short stays. Something about the place drew Emily in, a pull she couldn't quite explain.

Curious, she clicked on the listing to read more. The cottage was described as cosy and secluded, with two bedrooms, a small kitchen, and a sitting room with a fireplace. It was located on the outskirts of the village, offering privacy and tranquillity—exactly what Emily was looking for. Without hesitation, she clicked the "Book Now" button, feeling a sense of anticipation as she confirmed her reservation.

As she closed her laptop, Emily's gaze drifted to the folder on the counter. She couldn't help but wonder if there was more to this trip than just research. Something about Blackthorn Hollow seemed to be calling to her, drawing her in with a force she couldn't quite name. The cottage she had just booked felt like a part of that pull, as if it were waiting for her.

Shaking off the thought, Emily finished her coffee and began to prepare for the journey ahead. She packed a small suitcase with essentials, including her research materials and a few books on the history of witchcraft. As she zipped up the bag, she felt a strange mix of excitement and unease—emotions that had become all too familiar since discovering the Blackthorn sisters' story.

Before leaving, Emily sent a quick text to James, letting him know that she was on her way. *"Just booked a charming old cottage,"* she typed. *"I'll let you know how it is. Can't wait for you to join me."* His reply came almost immediately: *"Drive safe. I can't wait to be there with you. Love you."*

With that, Emily grabbed her suitcase and headed out the door, ready to embark on the next chapter of her research—and perhaps something more.

The drive to Blackthorn Hollow was tranquil, the peacefulness inviting contemplation. Emily navigated the winding country roads, the landscape unfurling before her like a series of picturesque scenes from a bygone era. Rolling hills blanketed in winter's light dusting of snow stretched out on either side, their gentle slopes dotted with clusters of trees that stood like silent sentinels in the crisp morning air. The winter sun hung low in the sky, casting long shadows across the fields, creating a patchwork of light and shade. As she drove south, the world around her seemed to slow down, the hustle and noise of city life fading into the background.

With each passing mile, Emily's thoughts drifted deeper into the mystery of Blackthorn Hollow. What secrets did the village hold? What remnants of the past lay hidden within its streets and buildings? She knew that history often left its mark on places as much as on people, and she wondered if Blackthorn Hollow would bear the weight of its history in the very air. It was a village nearly forgotten by time, its secrets buried deep, but Emily was determined to uncover them, to piece together the fragmented stories of those who had lived there.

As the hours passed, the road narrowed, winding through a dense forest where the trees grew close together, their bare branches interlocking overhead to create a canopy that filtered the weak winter sunlight. Emily felt a thrill of anticipation as her GPS announced that she was nearing her destination. The forest thinned out, revealing a small valley surrounded by hills, and there, nestled in the distance, was the village of Blackthorn Hollow. The sight was almost surreal, like returning to a place untouched by modernity.

Emily followed the GPS directions carefully, winding through the village's narrow streets. The houses she passed were old, their stone walls weathered by centuries of wind and rain, their thatched roofs sagging slightly under the weight of time. Though quaint and inviting, the village square was quiet, with only a few locals going about their day. There was a stillness to the place, a sense of quiet endurance as if the village had been waiting patiently through the ages for someone like her to arrive.

As she reached the outskirts of the village, Emily finally spotted the cottage from the listing—a small, charming stone building set back from the road, partially hidden by tall, ancient trees. It was even more enchanting in person, its ivy-covered walls giving it an aura of mystery and age. The gravel driveway crunched under her tyres as she pulled in, and she parked her car, taking a moment to absorb the scene before her. The air was crisp, tinged with pine and the faint aroma of wood smoke from some distant hearth. The quiet was almost palpable, broken only by the distant sound of birdsong and the occasional rustling of leaves in the breeze.

As she exited the car, Emily was greeted by an elderly woman emerging from behind the trees. She walked toward Emily with a warm smile, her movements slow but graceful, as if she were as much a part of the landscape as the trees and the cottage itself. She was petite, with a face lined with age but illuminated by bright eyes that sparkled with kindness. Her silver hair was pulled back into a neat bun, and she wore a thick woollen coat against the chill.

"Welcome to Blackthorn Hollow," the woman greeted, her voice as warm and welcoming as her smile. "You must be Dr. Ward. I'm Mrs. Whitaker. It's a pleasure to meet you."

Emily returned the smile, feeling an immediate sense of comfort in the woman's presence. "Thank you, Mrs. Whitaker. The pleasure is mine. The cottage is even more beautiful than I imagined."

Mrs Whitaker nodded, her eyes crinkling at the corners. "It's a special place, this cottage. It's been in the village for generations. We're lucky to have it still standing. Let me show you inside."

She led Emily to the front door, producing a large, old-fashioned key from her coat pocket. The key was a relic of another time, heavy and worn, its surface polished smooth from years of use. The door creaked slightly as it swung open, revealing a warm interior that smelled faintly of wood smoke and lavender. The walls were made of thick stone, and the floors were worn with wooden planks polished by time and countless footsteps. The furniture was a mix of old and new, with a large stone fireplace dominating the sitting room, its hearth stacked with neatly cut logs ready to be lit.

As they entered, Emily noticed a small table near the door, on which sat a welcome package. There was a bottle of red wine, a tin of biscuits, and a freshly baked loaf of bread wrapped in a cloth. A small note rested against the bottle, written in elegant script: "Welcome to Blackthorn Hollow. May your stay be peaceful and your heart light."

Mrs. Whitaker followed Emily's gaze and smiled. "It's a tradition in this cottage to leave a welcome package for every new visitor. An old custom of the house, you might say. A little something to help you settle in."

Emily felt a warmth spread through her at the gesture. "Thank you, Mrs. Whitaker. This is such a lovely surprise."

"You're most welcome, dear. If you need anything during your stay, I'm just down the road. Don't hesitate to call on me. The village is small, but it's full of friendly faces. I'm sure you'll find it quite to your liking."

As Mrs. Whitaker made her way to the door, she paused and looked back at Emily with a thoughtful expression. "This cottage has a lot of history, you know. Some say you can still feel it in the walls. I hope it brings you the peace you're looking for."

Emily nodded, her curiosity piqued by the older woman's words. "I'm sure it will. Thank you again for everything."

Mrs. Whitaker gave a final nod and left, the door closing softly behind her. Emily stood in the quiet of the cottage, taking in her surroundings. The room was warm and inviting, with the fire crackling softly in the hearth.

The scent of the bread and biscuits filled the air, mixing with the lingering fragrance of lavender. The cottage was simple but well-equipped, with everything she would need for her stay. As she unpacked her things, Emily couldn't shake the feeling that there was something familiar about the place that tugged at the edges of her memory.

She moved to the small kitchen, setting down her suitcase and placing the welcome package on the counter. The kitchen was charming, with its rustic wooden cabinets and old-fashioned appliances that seemed to belong to another era. A large window over the sink offered a view of the back garden, where a few hardy herbs still clung to life despite the winter cold. Emily could imagine spending quiet mornings here, sipping coffee and gazing at the serene landscape.

After unpacking, Emily poured herself a glass of wine from the welcome package and settled onto the sofa in the sitting room, letting the warmth of the fire seep into her bones. The day's events had left her both exhilarated and tired, but she couldn't help but feel she was exactly where she was meant to be. The journey had been long, but the anticipation that had carried her through it was still with her, now mingled with a deep sense of contentment.

She glanced around the room, her eyes lingering on the old wooden beams that crossed the ceiling and the thick stone walls that seemed to hum with a quiet, ancient energy. The sense of history Mrs Whitaker had mentioned was palpable, as if the cottage held memories of the lives that had passed through its doors. Emily felt a deep connection to the place, as if she had stepped into a story that had been waiting for her to arrive.

As the fire crackled softly and the winter evening deepened outside, Emily found her thoughts drifting back to the Blackthorn sisters. She didn't know much about them yet, but the fragments of their story she had uncovered were already weaving their way into her mind. The cottage felt like the perfect place to continue her research—where the past and present seemed to intertwine, where the echoes of history could be heard in the quiet of the night.

The warmth of the fire and the soft glow of the lamps created a cocoon of comfort around her, and Emily allowed herself to relax into the cushions, her eyes growing heavy. She would begin her exploration of the village tomorrow, but for now, she allowed herself to simply be, to feel the weight of the journey and the promise of what was to come. The welcome package had done its job, making her feel at home in this new and mysterious place.

As sleep began to overtake her, Emily thought she heard a faint whisper in the quiet of the room, a soft, almost imperceptible sound that seemed to come from the very walls of the cottage. It was a sound that spoke of age and memory, lives lived and stories untold. But before she could give it much thought, she drifted into a deep, dreamless sleep, the warmth of the fire and the ancient energy of the cottage wrapping around her like a protective cloak. The mystery of Blackthorn Hollow was waiting for her, and Emily knew she would be ready to face it when the time came.

THE FOLLOWING MORNING, Emily awoke to birds chirping outside her window, the soft light of dawn filtering through the curtains. For a moment, she lay still, letting the peacefulness of the cottage wash over her. The fire in the hearth had burned down to embers, and the room was cool but not uncomfortable. She felt rested and more at ease than she had in a long time, as if the cottage had worked its magic on her overnight.

After a leisurely breakfast of tea and toast with the fresh bread from the welcome package, Emily decided it was time to explore the village. Her thoughts were focused on the library, which she hoped would provide her with the information she needed to begin piecing together the history of Blackthorn Hollow. She had always found that the best way to start her research was by delving into the local archives, where the stories of a place were kept alive through records, letters, and old newspapers.

THE VILLAGE WAS HUSHED as Emily wandered through the narrow, winding streets, the crisp morning air sharpening her senses. The ancient buildings, with their half-timbered façades and crooked, thatched roofs, stood as silent witnesses to centuries of history. Each structure, with its weathered beams and leaded windows, seemed to murmur secrets of the past. The few villagers she encountered along the way offered polite nods, their expressions warm yet guarded, as if accustomed to the occasional outsider but content to keep their lives private. Emily found herself intrigued by these quiet inhabitants, curious about the stories and histories that lingered just beneath the surface of this timeless place.

The library stood in the heart of the village square, housed in a charming Tudor building with its half-timbered façade and uneven, sloping roof. Large, mullioned windows framed with dark wooden beams let the soft sunlight filter inside, casting a warm glow on the worn stone steps leading to the entrance. Above the heavy oak door, a sign hand-painted in an elegant script read "Lavenham Library and Historical Society." Emily felt a spark of excitement as she reached for the iron latch and stepped inside.

The library's interior was a cosy labyrinth of wooden shelves, each filled with a diverse collection of books, their spines well-worn from years of use. The familiar scent of old paper and polished oak permeated the air, wrapping Emily in comfort and nostalgia. Though the library was modest in size, it was impeccably maintained, with a small reading area near the front where a few villagers sat quietly, lost in their books beneath the soft light streaming in through the windows.

Emily made her way to the front desk, where a middle-aged woman with short, greying hair and kind eyes was typing away at a computer. She looked up as Emily approached, offering a friendly smile.

"Good morning," the woman greeted. "How can I help you today?"

"Good morning," Emily replied. "I'm Dr. Emily Ward, a historian. I'm researching the history of Blackthorn Hollow, and I was hoping to look through some of the archives."

The woman's smile widened, and she nodded in understanding. "Ah, we don't get many historians here, but we have a good local history collection. I'm Mrs. Fletcher, the librarian. I'd be happy to help you with anything you need."

"Thank you, Mrs. Fletcher," Emily said gratefully. "I'm particularly interested in any records or documents related to the village's history, especially around the late 16th century."

Mrs. Fletcher's expression becomes more thoughtful as she considers Emily's request. "The 16th century... yes, we have some records from that time, though they're sparse. The village has always been small, so not much was documented back then. But we have some old parish records, land deeds, and personal letters that might interest you. We also have some old maps and drawings of the village."

"That sounds perfect," Emily said, her excitement growing. "Where can I find these records?"

"I'll take you to the archives room," Mrs. Fletcher offered. "It's just down the hall. We keep the older documents there in a climate-controlled environment to preserve them. You're welcome to spend as much time there as you need."

Emily followed Mrs Fletcher down a narrow hallway lined with portraits of stern-looking men and women from centuries past. The librarian unlocked a door at the end of the hall, revealing a small room filled with filing cabinets, shelves of old books, and a large table in the centre where researchers could work.

"This is our archives room," Mrs. Fletcher said, gesturing. "It's not very large but holds some of the village's most valuable historical documents. If you need anything specific, just let me know. I'll be at the front desk."

"Thank you, Mrs. Fletcher," Emily said as she entered the room, her eyes scanning the shelves.

Mrs. Fletcher gave her a nod and left Emily to her work, closing the door softly behind her. Emily took a deep breath, feeling a sense of reverence as she stood in the small room. The air was cool and slightly musty, filled with the scent of old paper and leather-bound books. The shelves were lined with boxes and files, each labelled with dates and subjects that hinted at the wealth of information they contained.

Emily examined the old maps and drawings, carefully unrolling them on the large table. The maps were delicate, the paper yellowed with age, and the ink faded in places. She studied them closely, tracing the lines and landmarks with her finger, trying to match them with the current layout of the village. The drawings showed a familiar and different village, with buildings that no longer existed and pathways that time had overtaken.

As she worked, Emily felt a growing connection to the history of Blackthorn Hollow, as if the village itself were revealing its secrets to her. The more she learned, the more she realised that this place was not just a setting for her research but a key to understanding a part of history that had been largely forgotten.

After hours of poring over the documents, Emily was drawn to a small box labelled "Personal Correspondence: 16th Century." She discovered a bundle of letters tied with a faded ribbon, the paper fragile. She carefully untied the ribbon and began to read, the words penned by hands long gone, telling stories of life in Blackthorn Hollow during a time of fear and suspicion.

The letters were written by various villagers, recounting their daily lives, their struggles, and their fears. Some spoke of strange occurrences in the village—unexplained sicknesses, odd lights in the night, and the sense that something was not quite right. The tone of the letters grew more anxious as the years passed, hinting at an undercurrent of fear that seemed to permeate the village.

One letter, in particular, caught Emily's attention. It was addressed to a man named Thomas Grantham, a name she recognised from her previous research as a prominent figure in the village during the late 16th century.

Alice wrote the letter to express her concerns about the village's safety and the growing tension among the villagers.

"My dear Thomas," the letter began, "I write to you with a heavy heart, for I fear our village is in grave danger. The sickness that has spread through Blackthorn Hollow has taken many lives, and the people are growing restless. There are whispers of dark forces at work, and I fear we may face a threat that we do not fully understand. The villagers are looking for someone to blame, and I worry that their fear may lead to actions we will all regret..."

The letter continued, describing the unease over the village and the growing suspicion among the villagers. Emily felt a chill as she read, the words conveying a sense of dread that seemed to reach across the centuries. She knew this letter was a valuable piece of the puzzle, a glimpse into the mindset of the people who had lived in Blackthorn Hollow during a time of turmoil.

As the day wore on, Emily lost herself in the documents, piecing together the history of Blackthorn Hollow one fragment at a time. The more she learned, the more she realised that this village held more than just a story—a mystery that had yet to be fully uncovered.

When she finally emerged from the archives room, the sun had begun to set, casting long shadows across the village square. Mrs. Fletcher was still at the front desk, looking up with a smile as Emily approached.

"Did you find what you were looking for?" Mrs. Fletcher asked.

"I found more than I expected," Emily replied, her mind still buzzing with the information she had uncovered. "Thank you so much for your help. I'll definitely be back tomorrow to continue my research."

"Take your time," Mrs. Fletcher said kindly. "The history of Blackthorn Hollow is a deep well, and there's always more to discover."

As Emily stepped out into the cool evening air, she felt a sense of accomplishment mixed with anticipation. She had only scratched the surface of Blackthorn Hollow's history, but already she knew that this village held secrets waiting to be uncovered. The library had provided her with a wealth of information, but there was still much more to learn.

Emily returned to the cottage, her thoughts filled with the letters she had read and the stories they told. She knew she was on the brink of something significant that could change how history remembered this small, forgotten village. And as she settled into the warmth of the cottage that night, she felt a renewed sense of purpose, ready to dive even deeper into the mystery of Blackthorn Hollow.

Chapter Five: The Illness in Blackthorn Hollow

The Blackthorn sisters moved through the bustling village market with a sense of purpose, their woven baskets swinging at their sides as they navigated the crowded square. The market was lively, filled with the sounds of merchants hawking their goods, the chatter of villagers catching up on the latest news, and the occasional laughter of children darting between the stalls. The air was crisp with the promise of winter, but the sun's warmth still lingered, casting a golden glow over the scene.

Eliza, the eldest sister, led the way, her sharp eyes scanning the stalls for the needed herbs and supplies. Her dark hair was tied back neatly, and she wore a practical woollen cloak that brushed the ground as she walked. Ever the nurturing presence, Margaret was beside her, her hazel eyes filled with their usual warmth as she greeted the villagers they passed. Anne, the youngest, trailed behind, her auburn hair catching the sunlight as she lingered at a stall selling brightly coloured ribbons, her green eyes alight with interest.

The market was a familiar place to the sisters, a central part of life in Blackthorn Hollow where they could gather the materials for their work and the news of the village. Today, however, there was an undercurrent of tension in the air, a subtle shift in the atmosphere that made the sisters exchange uneasy glances.

As they made their way to the herbalist's stall, they overheard snippets of conversation that sent a chill through them.

"Did you hear about little Jack?" one woman whispered to another, her voice low and anxious. "He's taken ill, just like the Miller's boy."

"Another one?" the second woman replied, her tone sharp with concern. "That's the fifth child this week. What's happening to our village?"

The sisters paused, their attention caught by the conversation. Eliza frowned, a deep crease forming between her brows. "It's spreading," she murmured to Margaret, her voice just above a whisper. "More children are falling ill."

Margaret nodded, her expression troubled. "We need to find out what's causing this. The remedies we've been preparing aren't enough. Something more is at work here."

Anne, who had been listening quietly, moved closer to her sisters, her eyes wide with worry. "Do you think it's something in the water? Or maybe a sickness carried by the wind?"

"We won't know until we investigate further," Eliza replied, her voice firm. "But we need to act quickly before more children fall ill."

The sisters continued through the market, gathering the needed supplies while keeping their ears open for any news. As they moved from stall to stall, they could feel the eyes of the villagers on them, some filled with hope, others with a growing sense of unease. The Blackthorn sisters had always been the ones to turn to in need. Their knowledge of herbs and healing was a source of comfort for the village. But as the illness spread, that trust was beginning to waver.

After collecting their supplies, the sisters went to the village square to speak with the other villagers. They knew they needed to gather as much information as possible to have any hope of stopping the illness. As they approached a group of women huddled near the well, they noticed the worried expressions on their faces.

"Good morning, Mrs. Hartwell," Margaret greeted one of the women, her voice gentle. "How is your son doing? I heard he's been unwell."

Mrs. Hartwell, a middle-aged woman with worry etched into her features, looked up at Margaret, her eyes filled with fear. "He's still sick, I'm afraid. The fever hasn't broken, and he's so weak. I don't know what to do."

"We'll come by later to check on him," Eliza offered, her tone reassuring. "Has he been near anything unusual? Playing in a new area, perhaps?"

Mrs. Hartwell shook her head. "No, he's been at home most days, helping his father. But the fever came on suddenly, and now he can barely get out of bed."

Eliza exchanged a concerned glance with her sisters. "We'll do everything we can," she promised, her voice steady. "We need to understand what's causing this so we can stop it."

As the sisters moved on, they gathered similar stories from other villagers. The illness seemed to strike without warning, leaving the children weak and feverish, their bodies wracked with chills. No one could pinpoint the cause, and the remedies that had always worked before seemed powerless against this new affliction.

The sisters knew they had to act quickly. The market, usually a place of bustling activity and cheerful exchanges, now felt heavy with fear. The villagers' eyes followed the sisters as they made their way to the square's edge, their expressions a mixture of hope and desperation.

"We need to visit the families of the sick children," Eliza said as they left the market behind. "We need to see for ourselves what's happening."

The sisters went through the village, stopping first at the Hartwell home. The small cottage was neat and well-kept, but the air inside was thick with the scent of sickness. Young Thomas Hartwell lay on a cot near the hearth, his face pale and breathing laboured. Margaret knelt beside him, her hands gentle as she checked his temperature and felt his pulse.

"He's burning up," Margaret said quietly, her concern deepening. "We need to get this fever down."

Anne moved to the small table where the family kept their modest supplies, gathering the herbs they had brought from the market. "I'll make a poultice," she said, her voice determined. "It should help with the fever."

Eliza, meanwhile, questioned Mrs Hartwell further, trying to piece together any clues that might explain the sudden spread of the illness.

"Has anyone else in the family been ill? Or have you noticed anything unusual around the village?"

Mrs. Hartwell shook her head, her eyes filled with tears. "No, nothing like that. It's just the children. I don't understand what's happening. We've always been healthy, but now..."

Eliza placed a comforting hand on her shoulder. "We'll find out what's causing this, I promise. We won't let it spread any further."

The sisters worked quickly, preparing the poultice and applying it to the boy's chest, hoping to draw out the fever. They stayed with the family longer, offering what comfort they could before moving on to the next home.

It was the same story at each house they visited. The children were weak, their bodies fighting a fever that refused to break. The parents were worried, their faith in the sisters' abilities wavering. The illness was spreading faster than anyone had expected, and the sisters knew they were running out of time.

The sisters returned to their cottage as the sun began to set, casting long shadows across the village. The weight of the day's events hung heavy in the air, the usual warmth of their home feeling dimmed by the fear gripping the village.

"We have to find out what's causing this," Margaret said as they sat around the kitchen table, their faces etched with worry. "The usual remedies aren't working. There has to be something we're missing."

Eliza nodded, her mind racing with possibilities. "We need to consider everything. Where have the children been playing? What have they eaten? Has anything changed in the village recently?"

"I've heard some of the children have been playing near the old mill," Anne said, her voice thoughtful. "Maybe there's something there that we haven't seen yet."

Eliza considered this, her expression serious. "It's worth investigating. We'll go there tomorrow and see if we can find any clues."

The sisters spent the rest of the evening discussing their plan, determined to uncover the cause of the illness. They knew that the village depended on them and couldn't afford to fail. As they prepared for bed, the usual comfort of their routine was overshadowed by the growing sense of urgency.

The following day, the sisters set out for the old mill, their hearts heavy with worry but bolstered by a strong resolve. The path to the mill was narrow and overgrown, with weeds and brambles snagging at their skirts as they made their way through. The air was thick with the scent of damp earth and decaying leaves, while the gnarled trees on either side seemed to close around them, their bare branches intertwining to form a canopy that cast long, eerie shadows on the ground.

It stood as a forlorn relic of a bygone era when they reached the mill. The once-sturdy wooden beams had begun to rot, sagging and splintered in places, while the old stone walls were cloaked in a thick layer of moss and lichen, giving the building a greenish hue. The large waterwheel, which had once turned with steady purpose, now hung crookedly in the slow-moving stream, its timbers creaking and groaning with each sluggish rotation. The symbol of the village's industrious spirit now stood as a ghost of its former self, a silent testament to the passage of time and neglect.

The sisters moved cautiously, their eyes scanning the area for anything causing the sickness. They searched the ground for strange plants or fungi, checked the water for signs of contamination, and even examined the walls of the mill for mould or rot that could be affecting the children.

After a thorough search, they found nothing that could explain the illness. The area around the mill was deserted, and though it was eerie in its neglect, there was nothing overtly dangerous about it.

"Maybe we're looking in the wrong place," Anne said, her voice tinged with frustration. "What if it's something else entirely?"

"We'll keep looking," Eliza replied, her tone determined. "If it's not the mill, it must be something else in the village. We can't give up."

The sisters returned to the village, their minds heavy with worry. As they walked through the streets, they could feel the eyes of the villagers on them, the weight of their expectations pressing down on them. The sisters had always been the healers of the village, the ones people turned to in times of need, but now they felt powerless in the face of an illness they could not understand.

As the days passed, the situation in Blackthorn Hollow grew more dire. More children fell ill, and the fear among the villagers began to turn to suspicion. Whispers started to spread, whispers that the illness was not natural, that there was something darker at work in the village. Some even suggested that the sisters might be involved, that their knowledge of herbs and healing was somehow connected to the sickness ravaging the village.

The sisters could feel the change in the air, the way the villagers' eyes would linger on them a moment too long, the way conversations would hush when they approached. The fear was palpable, and it was turning the villagers against them.

The Blackthorn sisters had barely returned to their cottage after the unsettling visit to the old mill when there was a frantic knock at their door. The sound echoed through the quiet house, startling them from their thoughts. Eliza was the first to reach the door, her heart already heavy with the weight of the day's events. When she opened it, she found a young man standing there, his face pale and lined with fear.

"Please, you must come quickly," he gasped, his voice trembling. "It's the Vaughan children—they've both fallen ill."

Eliza's eyes widened in alarm. "We'll come at once," she said, turning back to her sisters, who had already gathered their supplies, their faces reflecting Eliza's same concern.

The Vaughan family was well-known in Blackthorn Hollow and respected for their generosity and involvement in the village's affairs. Mr Vaughan was a kind man, and his wife, Mrs. Vaughan, was known for her gentle nature. Their two children, Thomas and Mary, were lively and bright, always seen playing in the village square or helping their mother with chores. The news that both children had fallen ill sent a shiver down Eliza's spine.

The sisters quickly gathered what they needed—herbs, tinctures, and poultices they had prepared earlier—and hurried out the door. The sun was setting, casting long shadows across the village as they made their way to the Vaughan house. The wind had picked up, carrying the scent of wood smoke and the faintest hint of winter's chill.

The Vaughan house was one of the larger homes in the village, with sturdy stone walls and a well-tended garden that was now bare and waiting for the spring. As the sisters approached, they could see the flicker of candlelight in the windows and hear the low murmur of voices from within. The atmosphere was heavy with dread, which settles over a household when illness takes hold.

Mrs. Vaughan met them at the door, her face drawn with worry. "Thank you for coming," she said, her voice barely above a whisper. "I didn't know where else to turn."

"Tell us what's happened," Eliza urged gently, her tone reassuring.

Mrs. Vaughan led them into the house, her hands trembling as she spoke. "It started this morning. At first, Thomas complained of feeling tired, then he developed a fever. By midday, Mary was the same. They're both so weak now, and their skin... it's covered in a rash, red and angry."

Eliza exchanged a look with Margaret and Anne, her concern deepening. A rash could mean many things, but with the fever and weakness, one illness immediately came to mind—smallpox.

"Show us to the children," Margaret said softly, her voice calm despite her fear.

Mrs Vaughan led them upstairs to a small bedroom where the two children lay in their beds, side by side. The room was dim, lit only by a few candles, and the air was thick with the smell of illness. Thomas, the elder of the two at nine years old, was lying still, his face flushed with fever, his breathing shallow. Mary, who was only six months old, lay beside him, her small body curled up under the blankets, her cheeks burning with the same fever. Both children's faces and arms were marked with a red, raised rash, the unmistakable sign of smallpox.

Eliza's heart sank as she took in the scene. She had feared this might be the cause of the illness spreading through the village, but seeing it confirmed in the Vaughan children brought a deep sense of dread. Smallpox was a dangerous and often deadly disease, and with it spreading among the children, the entire village was at risk.

Margaret immediately knelt beside Thomas, placing a cool hand on his forehead. "He's burning up," she murmured, reaching for the tinctures they had brought. "We need to bring his fever down."

Anne moved to Mary's side, her fingers trembling slightly as she checked the girl's pulse. "She's so weak," Anne whispered, her green eyes filled with worry. "We need to act quickly."

Eliza, meanwhile, took Mrs. Vaughan aside, her voice gentle but firm.

"This is smallpox. We've seen it before, though never this severe. We'll do everything we can, but you need to know this is a serious illness. It can spread quickly, especially to those without it before."

Mrs. Vaughan's face went even paler, her eyes wide with fear. "Smallpox? But... how did they get it? We've been so careful. They haven't been near anyone who was sick."

"It could have come from anything—something they touched or even the air," Eliza explained, though she knew the truth was more complex. Smallpox was a disease that could spread insidiously, often appearing without warning and leaving devastation in its wake.

"We need to isolate them as much as possible," Eliza continued. "No one else should enter this room except you and Mr. Vaughan. And even then, you must be careful. Wash your hands thoroughly, and don't touch your face after being near them."

Mrs Vaughan nodded, tears welling in her eyes. "What will happen to them?"

Eliza hesitated, knowing she couldn't offer the reassurance Mrs. Vaughan so desperately wanted. "We'll do our best," she said finally. "We'll treat the fever and the rash, and we'll monitor them closely. But smallpox is unpredictable. We must prepare for whatever may come."

Mrs Vaughan covered her mouth with her hand, her shoulders trembling as she fought to hold back her sobs. Eliza placed a comforting hand on her arm, offering what little solace she could.

"Stay strong for them," Eliza said softly. "They need you now more than ever."

Returning to the children's bedside, Eliza joined her sisters in their work. They brewed a strong tea from willow bark to help reduce the fever and prepared a soothing poultice of chamomile and lavender to apply to the rash. The sisters worked in silence, their usual rhythm of cooperation now tinged with the situation's urgency.

As they tended to the children, Eliza couldn't help but think of the other families in the village, the children who might face the same fate. If smallpox had taken hold in Blackthorn Hollow, there was no telling how far it might spread.

"We need to warn the rest of the village," Eliza said quietly, glancing at her sisters. "They need to know what we're dealing with."

Margaret nodded in agreement, her face set in determination. "We'll go door to door if we have to. They need to be prepared."

Anne's voice was soft but steady as she added, "We'll do whatever it takes. We won't let this destroy our village."

As the night wore on, the sisters stayed with the Vaughan children, administering the remedies and keeping a close eye on their condition. The fever showed no signs of breaking, and the rash seemed to worsen, the angry red welts spreading across their skin. Mrs Vaughan sat by the window, her hands clasped tightly in her lap, her eyes never leaving her children.

The hours passed slowly, each minute weighed down by the tension in the room. The sisters took turns resting briefly in the chairs by the fire, but none of them could truly sleep, their minds too occupied with the gravity of the situation.

By the time the first light of dawn began to filter through the window, the children's condition had not improved. Their breathing remained shallow, their skin hot to the touch. The sisters knew they had done all they could for the moment, but the uncertainty hung over them like a cloud.

"We'll be back later today," Eliza said to Mrs. Vaughan as they prepared to leave. "Keep them comfortable, and don't hesitate to send for us if anything changes."

Mrs Vaughan nodded, her voice choked with emotion. "Thank you... thank you for everything."

The sisters left the Vaughan house in silence, the weight of the illness pressing down on them. The village was still quiet in the early morning light, and the streets were empty as the day began. But the sisters knew that Blackthorn Hollow was far from peaceful now. The shadow of smallpox had fallen over the village, and the fear was growing with each passing hour.

As they returned to their cottage, the sisters shared a heavy silence. There was so much more to do, so many more families to warn, but the task felt overwhelming. The illness was spreading faster than they could contain it, and the villagers were looking to them for answers they might be unable to provide.

"We have to be strong," Margaret said finally, her voice breaking the silence. "The village needs us now more than ever."

Eliza nodded, her resolve hardening. "We'll do everything in our power to stop this. We can't give up."

Anne, always the optimist, managed a small, hopeful smile. "We'll get through this, just like we always have. Together."

The sisters exchanged a determined glance, their bond as strong as ever. They had faced challenges before, but this was different. The illness was relentless, and the fear it had sown was even more dangerous. But they would stand firm, just as they always had, because Blackthorn Hollow was their home, and they would protect it with everything they had.

As they reached the door of their cottage, Eliza paused, turning to look back at the village. The sun was rising, casting a soft light over the rooftops and the trees, but the beauty of the morning was lost on her. She could only think of the Vaughan children, lying weak and feverish in their beds, and the other families who might soon face the same fate.

"We'll start with the closest families," Eliza said, her voice resolute. "We'll warn them and do what we can to keep this from spreading. We can't afford to lose any more time."

Margaret and Anne nodded in agreement, their expressions mirroring Eliza's determination. They knew the road ahead would be difficult, but they were ready to face whatever came their way. Together, they would do everything possible to protect the village and the people they loved.

Chapter Six: The Sisters Speak

The wind howled outside, its fierce gusts rattling the leaded windows of the cottage as Emily Ward sat at the sturdy oak table in the kitchen, poring over her notes. The uneven timber beams, dark with age, crisscrossed the whitewashed walls, giving the interior a rustic elegance. The thick thatched roof, now sagging slightly under the weight of centuries, added to the cottage's enchanting, fairy-tale appearance, though it did little to keep out the biting cold that crept in from every corner.

The fireplace, built from ancient, uneven stones and blackened from years of use, cast a flickering, warm glow across the room, but it did little to chase away the deep chill that had settled in Emily's bones since her return to Blackthorn Hollow. The cottage, which had initially seemed so quaint and welcoming, now felt like a place steeped in memory, where the past clung to every shadow and whispered in the drafty hallways. The once-inviting space had taken on an eerie stillness, as if the very walls held onto secrets that refused to be forgotten, leaving Emily with a sense of unease that only grew with each passing day.

Books she had carefully placed on her desk ended up on the floor, their pages splayed open as if someone had been reading them. The kettle she had left on the stove was suddenly on the counter, its contents untouched and cold. Even the curtains, which she distinctly remembered closing before bed, would be found slightly ajar in the morning, allowing the pale dawn light to filter into the room.

Tonight, the feeling was powerful. As she sat at the kitchen table, trying to focus on the trial records she had brought from the library, Emily couldn't shake the sensation that she was not alone. The hair on the back of her neck prickled, and every creak of the floorboards echoed louder than it should have.

At first, Emily tried to rationalise it all—perhaps she was simply more tired than she realised, her mind playing tricks on her in the quiet of the old cottage.

But soon, the unsettling feeling became impossible to ignore. There were other, more disturbing signs as well: the faint rustling of fabric when no one else was around, the subtle creak of floorboards as though someone was walking just out of sight, and those fleeting shadows that danced at the corners of her vision, disappearing the moment she turned to face them.

What had once seemed like a cosy and charming retreat now felt oppressive, as if the walls were closing in on her. With its ivy-covered walls and rustic charm, the cottage was beginning to reveal its secrets in ways that left Emily both intrigued and deeply unnerved.

Emily forced herself to concentrate on the documents in front of her. She was determined to understand what had happened to the Blackthorn sisters—to uncover the truth behind their tragic story. But the words on the pages blurred together, her mind unable to stay focused. Each time she tried to read, her thoughts drifted back to the strange occurrences in the cottage, the feeling that she was not alone, and the oppressive sense of dread that seemed to grow stronger with each passing day.

Finally, she gave up, closing the book with a sigh and rubbing her tired eyes. The hour was late, and the cottage was filled with an eerie quiet, broken only by the occasional creak of the old wooden beams and the soft whistle of the wind outside. Exhausted and unnerved, Emily turned in for the night, hoping that sleep would bring her some respite.

Upstairs, the bedrooms are nestled beneath high, sloping roofs, their ceilings crisscrossed with exposed timber beams that evoke a rustic, historical charm. The rooms are small but warm, filled with simple, sturdy furnishings that reflect the cottage's age and the lives of those who have called it home. Despite the passage of time, the Blackthorn sisters' cottage has been lovingly maintained, blending its rich history with the necessities of daily life. Each room feels both ancient and alive, a sanctuary steeped in past mysteries.

As she made her way to the bedroom, the soft glow of the bedside lamp cast long, wavering shadows on the walls, dancing across the beams overhead. The room felt intimate and close, the ceiling seeming to press down as if the weight of the years was settling around her. Climbing into bed, Emily couldn't shake the unsettling sensation of the room closing in, the darkness pressing down like a heavy blanket. She pulled the covers tightly up to her chin and closed her eyes, trying to will herself to sleep, but the feeling of the past lingering in the corners of the room refused to let her mind rest.

But when sleep finally came, it was anything but restful.

In her dreams, Emily stood in the middle of Blackthorn Hollow, the village square deserted and bathed in an unnatural light. The air was thick with tension, and she could hear the distant murmur of voices—angry, fearful, accusing. She tried to move, but her feet felt rooted, trapped in some invisible force.

Suddenly, the scene shifted, and she was inside a dark, damp cell. The walls were cold and slick with moisture, and the only light came from a small, barred window high above. The air was heavy with the stench of fear and despair, and Emily realised with a jolt that she was no longer herself—she was one of the Blackthorn sisters, locked away in this wretched place, waiting for a fate she knew she could not escape.

She could hear metal clanging as the cell door was wrenched open, and a figure stepped inside, casting a long shadow across the stone floor. It was Sir Edward Grantham, his face twisted with malice and satisfaction. His eyes bore into her, filled with cold cruelty as he delivered the sentence that sealed her fate.

"You and your sisters are to be hanged at dawn," he said, his voice dripping with contempt. "For the crimes of witchcraft, for the curses you have placed upon this village."

Emily—no, Eliza—felt her heart pound in her chest, a mix of fear and anger surging through her. She wanted to scream, lash out, and tell him that they were innocent, that they had only ever used their knowledge to heal, to help. But her voice was silent, trapped within the nightmare that felt all too real.

The scene shifted again, and Emily found herself in the village square again, surrounded by a jeering crowd. The villagers' faces were twisted with fear and hatred, their voices rising in a crescendo of accusations and curses. She could feel the rough noose around her neck, the scratchy rope biting into her skin as she stood on the wooden platform, her hands bound in front of her.

She saw Margaret and Anne beside her, their faces pale but resolute, their eyes filled with the same mix of terror and defiance that she felt. The three of them were united in their final moments, a bond forged in blood and injustice.

The last thing Emily saw before everything went black was Sir Edward Grantham's face, standing in front of the crowd, his cold eyes gleaming with triumph as he gave the signal.

Emily woke with a start, her heart pounding and her breath coming in short, panicked gasps. The room was dark, the shadows deep and menacing. She couldn't tell momentarily if she was still in the dream or had woken up.

Then, without warning, a loud crash echoed from above, jolting her fully awake. The sound seemed to come from the attic, where she had found the journal only hours before. The noise was sudden and violent as if something heavy had been thrown across the floor.

Adrenaline surged through her as she threw off the covers and jumped out of bed. Her heart raced, a mix of fear and curiosity driving her forward. She grabbed the flashlight from the bedside table, its beam cutting through the darkness as she hurried toward the attic.

The narrow staircase creaked ominously as she ascended, each step feeling heavier than the last. The door to the attic was slightly ajar, just as it had been when she found the journal. Emily hesitated momentarily, her hand hovering over the doorknob as she steeled herself for whatever she might find on the other side.

With a deep breath, she pushed the door open, the hinges groaning in protest. The attic was dark and cold, the only light coming from the narrow beam of her flashlight. She swept the light across the room, her eyes scanning for the source of the noise.

But it was the silence that unnerved her the most. The noise that had brought her up here had ceased as abruptly as it had begun, leaving only the sound of her own breathing to break the stillness.

At first, everything seemed as it had been—dusty old boxes, forgotten trunks, and the remnants of a life-long past. But then Emily noticed a book lying in the middle of the floor, its pages splayed open as if it had been flung. Emily's heart skipped a beat as she recognised it immediately. It was the same journal she had found earlier, which belonged to the Blackthorn sisters.

Slowly, she approached the book, her hand trembling as she reached down to pick it up. As soon as her fingers touched the leather cover, a chill ran down her spine, and the temperature in the room seemed to drop even further.

The first few pages were filled with detailed descriptions of various plants and their medicinal properties and instructions on preparing them for healing. Emily's heart raced as she realised what she was holding—this was a record of the sisters' work, their knowledge passed down through generations, hidden away for centuries.

But as she turned the pages, the entries became less clinical and more personal. The neat script gave way to hurried, frantic writing, as if the author had been trying to record her thoughts as quickly as possible. Emily could almost feel the fear and desperation in the words, the growing sense of dread as the sisters realised what was happening in the village.

One entry, in particular, caught Emily's attention. It was dated just days before the sisters were arrested, and the handwriting was shaky, the ink smudged in places as if it had been written in haste:

They are coming for us. The whispers have grown louder, and they look more hostile. We have done nothing but heal and help those in need, but they do not understand. They see only what they fear. I fear for what will come. I fear for our lives. We have done no wrong, but I know that will not save us.

Emily's hands shook as she read the words, feeling a cold dread settle over her. The sisters knew they were in danger, and the village turned against them. But there was nothing they could do to stop it.

She continued reading, her eyes scanning the pages as quickly as possible. The journal described how the sisters had been accused of cursing the village and how their healing practices had been twisted into something dark and sinister by those who didn't understand. The local magistrate, Sir Edward Grantham, had driven the accusations, using the villagers' fear to fuel his vendetta against the sisters.

The trial, as Emily had already suspected, had been a farce. The sisters had pleaded their innocence, but their words had fallen on deaf ears. The verdict was inevitable—they were found guilty of witchcraft and sentenced to death by hanging.

The final entries in the journal were the most harrowing. The sisters had spent their last days in a cold, dark cell, awaiting their execution. They had been terrified but also found strength in each other, determined to face their fate with dignity. Their last words, written in a trembling hand, were a plea for justice:

If there is any justice in this world, let it be known that we are innocent. Let the truth come to light, and let those who wronged us be held accountable. We do not curse this village, but we curse those who would see us dead for their own gain. Let our spirits find peace, and let our story be told.

Emily's vision blurred with tears as she read the final words. The sisters had been innocent; their only crime was their knowledge of healing and refusal to bow to ignorance and fear. And now, centuries later, their spirits were still restless, still seeking the justice that had been denied them.

A sudden chill swept through the attic, and Emily felt a presence behind her. She turned, her heart pounding in her chest, but nothing was there—only the shadows dancing on the walls, flickering in the dim light.

But as she stood there, she felt a hand brush against her shoulder, cold and soft as a whisper. She gasped, dropping the journal, and the flashlight slipped from her grasp, plunging the room into darkness. The shadows seemed to close in around her, the cold growing more intense as if the very air was being sucked from the room.

Then, out of the darkness, she saw them—faint, ghostly shapes forming slowly before her eyes. Three pale and translucent figures stood in the attic with her, their faces shadowed but unmistakable. The Blackthorn sisters were there, watching her, their expressions a mix of sorrow, fear, and an unyielding plea for justice.

Emily clutched the journal to her chest, her voice barely a whisper as she addressed the spirits. "What do you want from me?"

She knew who they were. She had seen their faces in her dreams and heard their voices in the whispers that haunted the cottage. The Blackthorn sisters were here, their spirits bound to this place, their story etched into the very walls of the cottage.

For a moment, Emily was paralysed with fear, unable to move or speak. But then one of the figures stepped forward, her face coming into view. It was Eliza, the eldest sister, her dark eyes filled with sorrow and pain. She reached out a hand, and Emily felt a rush of cold air as it passed through her.

The figures didn't speak, but their presence was overwhelming. Emily felt their emotions as if they were her own—rage at the injustice that had been done to them, grief for the lives that had been stolen, and a desperate need to be heard, to be understood.

The attic seemed to close in around her, the air thick with the weight of centuries-old pain and suffering. Emily felt tears spring, her heart aching for the sisters who had endured so much.

As she stood there, trembling in the darkness, the sisters seemed to draw closer, their forms becoming clearer. She could see their faces now—Eliza's stern determination, Margaret's gentle sorrow, and Anne's quiet, lingering fear. They reached out to her, their hands ghostly and cold but filled with a silent plea.

"You found us," Eliza whispered, her voice barely audible above the wind that howled through the attic. "You know the truth."

Emily nodded, tears streaming down her face. "I'm so sorry," she whispered, her voice breaking. "I'm so sorry for what happened to you."

Eliza's expression softened, and she nodded slowly. "It was not your doing. But now you must help us. Our story must be told."

"I will," Emily promised, her voice trembling. "I'll make sure everyone knows what happened. I'll bring your story to light."

The other two sisters stepped forward, their faces pale and ghostly in the dim light. Margaret, the middle sister, placed a hand on Eliza's shoulder, and Anne, the youngest, reached out to Emily, her touch sending a jolt of cold through her body.

"We are trapped here," Anne said softly, her voice filled with sadness. "We cannot move on until justice is done."

Emily nodded, her heart breaking for the sisters who had suffered so much. "I'll do everything I can," she said, her voice steady despite the fear that gripped her. "I'll find the evidence to clear your names. I'll ensure Sir Edward Grantham's crimes are exposed for what they truly were."

Eliza's spectral form seemed to soften at Emily's words, her ghostly eyes filled with a sorrow that had lingered for centuries. Margaret, standing beside her, offered a faint smile of gratitude while Anne's ethereal hand briefly brushed against Emily's, a touch that was both cold and comforting.

"Thank you," Eliza whispered, her voice like a breeze rustling through leaves. "We've waited so long..."

And then, just as suddenly as they had appeared, the sisters were gone, leaving Emily alone in the attic again. The flashlight flickered back to life, its beam cutting through the darkness, and the oppressive chill lifted.

Emily stood there momentarily, the journal still clutched in her hands, her mind reeling from what she had just experienced. She knew now, without a doubt, that the Blackthorn sisters were with her, guiding her, and that their story was far from over.

She took a deep breath, her resolve hardening as she turned to leave the attic. Much work was to be done, and the sisters were counting on her. With the journal in hand and the memory of their presence still fresh, Emily descended the stairs, ready to face whatever lay ahead.

Chapter Seven: The Hammer Falls

The winter wind howled through the narrow streets of Blackthorn Hollow, carrying with it the cold bite of fear that had settled over the village. The sky was a dull, oppressive grey, heavy with the threat of snow, and the usual bustle of the village square was subdued, the villagers huddled together in hushed conversations, their faces pale and anxious.

At the square's edge, the Blackthorn sisters went about their work with a quiet determination, their expressions carefully neutral as they sensed the growing unease around them. Eliza, Margaret, and Anne had noticed the change in the village over the past weeks—the suspicious glances, the whispered accusations—but they had hoped it would pass, that reason would prevail.

But today, the tension in the air was palpable, and the sisters knew that something was coming—something dark and dangerous.

Their fears were confirmed when a group of men rode into the village, their arrival announced by the clatter of hooves on cobblestones and the ominous sound of the church bell tolling in the distance. The men were strangers, their presence immediately commanding attention as they dismounted and strode into the square, their expressions grim and resolute.

At their head was a tall, stern-looking man with a hawk-like face and cold, calculating eyes. He carried an air of authority, his every movement purposeful and deliberate. The villagers parted before him, their eyes wide with fear and awe as they watched him approach.

Eliza exchanged a glance with Margaret and Anne, her heart sinking. She recognised the man from descriptions she had heard in passing—Sir Edward Grantham, the local magistrate, known for his ruthless enforcement of the law and his unwavering belief in the dangers of witchcraft.

Behind Sir, Edward walked two men whose presence sent a chill down Eliza's spine. The first was Matthew Hopkins, the self-proclaimed Witchfinder

General, a figure who had become notorious for his relentless persecution of women accused of witchcraft. His thin, angular face was set in a permanent scowl, and his eyes, cold and calculating, seemed to miss nothing. Beside him was John Stearne, his trusted associate, a stocky man with a cruel mouth and a reputation for extracting confessions through any means necessary.

The other men were members of his retinue, all armed and dressed in dark, sombre clothing that matched the day's mood. They spread across the square, their eyes scanning the crowd as if searching for something—or someone.

"Gather the villagers," Sir Edward commanded, his voice cold and authoritative. "There are matters to discuss."

The village elder, a frail man with thinning white hair, stepped forward hesitantly. "Sir Edward, what brings you to Blackthorn Hollow?" he asked, his voice trembling slightly.

Sir Edward fixed him with a hard stare. "Rumors of witchcraft," he replied, his tone leaving no room for doubt. "There have been reports of unnatural occurrences, of crops failing and children dying. This village is under suspicion, and we are here to make inquiries."

A murmur of fear rippled through the crowd, the villagers exchanging worried glances. The word "witchcraft" carried a heavy weight, especially in these times of uncertainty and fear. The unease in the square was palpable, a tension thickening as every pair of eyes slowly turned toward the Blackthorn sisters.

Whispers spread like wildfire through the crowd, growing louder with each passing second. "It's them," someone muttered, the words laced with fear and accusation. "The Blackthorn sisters—it's their doing."

Among the villagers, the young girl who had first spoken up—Beatrice Turner, the farmer's daughter—stared wide-eyed at the sisters. Her face was pale, her lips trembling as she clutched at her father's sleeve. Encouraged by the murmurs around her, she pointed a trembling finger at Eliza, Margaret, and Anne, her voice breaking as she spoke.

"It's them!" Beatrice cried out, her tiny voice cutting through the hushed tension. "They're the ones! They're the witches!"

Her words hit the sisters like a physical blow. Eliza felt her breath catch in her throat, a cold dread settling over her as she saw the tide of fear turn against them. The whispers grew louder, more insistent, as the villagers seized upon the child's words. She could see the fear in the villagers' eyes, the way they looked at her and her sisters as if they were already condemned. The accusations were baseless, born of ignorance and superstition, but she knew how quickly such fears could spiral out of control.

"Their herbs bring death, not healing!" shouted a man from the back of the crowd, his voice trembling with a mix of fear and anger. "My crops failed after I took their remedy!"

Another voice chimed in, a woman clutching her young son to her chest. "My child fell ill after they treated him! They've cursed us all!"

The accusations echoed through the square, fueled by the villagers' growing hysteria. The Blackthorn sisters stood rooted to the spot, the weight of the crowd's fear and suspicion pressing down on them like a suffocating fog. The people they had spent their lives caring for, healing, and helping were now turning against them, driven by a terror they could not control.

"They've brought this curse upon us!" an older woman cried out, her voice shaking with emotion. "It's them—the witches!"

As the accusations swirled around them, the sisters exchanged a glance, a silent understanding passing between them. They had always known there was a risk in their work, a danger that came with the knowledge they carried. But they had never imagined it would come to this—standing before their own people, accused of what they had fought against all their lives.

Eliza stepped forward, her voice strong despite the turmoil inside her. "We are not witches," she said firmly, her gaze sweeping the crowd. "We are healers. We've done nothing but try to help you all."

But her words were drowned out by the rising tide of fear and anger, the villagers too consumed by their terror to listen to reason. The crowd began to close in around them, their faces twisted with a mix of horror and rage as if the very sight of the sisters had become unbearable.

"It's their fault the children are dying!" someone shouted.

"They've cursed the village!"

"The Blackthorn sisters are witches!"

"We have done nothing wrong," Margaret said quietly, her voice steady despite the tension in the air. "Our only crime is that we know how to heal, and now they use that against us."

As the shouts grew louder and frenzied, Eliza felt a shiver run down her spine. The air crackled with the energy of the crowd's fear, and she knew, with a sinking heart, that there was no reasoning with them now. The seeds of doubt and suspicion had been planted and took root, growing into a deadly force that threatened to destroy everything the sisters had worked for.

Anne nodded in agreement, her usually bright and lively eyes now clouded with worry. "But how can we defend ourselves against lies and fear?"

Eliza shook her head. Her heart was heavy, knowing there might be no defence against what was coming. "We must remain strong," she said softly. "We cannot let fear dictate our actions. We will face this together."

Suddenly, Sir Edward Grantham stepped forward, his cold eyes gleaming with a dangerous resolve. He raised his hand, and the crowd fell silent, their anger and fear now focused entirely on the sisters.

"The evidence is clear," Sir Edward declared, his voice ringing over the square. "The Blackthorn sisters have brought this curse upon the village. They must answer for their crimes."

The crowd erupted in cheers and shouts of agreement, their voices merging into a deafening roar of condemnation. Eliza's heart pounded in her chest as she realised the full extent of their danger. Sir Edward had decided, and the villagers were ready to follow him, no matter the cost.

As the crowd surged forward, intent on seizing the sisters, Eliza knew their fate was sealed. The fear gripping the village had now turned into a weapon that would be wielded against them with deadly precision.

As the villagers closed in, their faces twisted with anger and fear, Eliza could only pray that, somehow, the truth would be revealed before it was too late.

But there was no time to plead or reason. Rough hands grabbed hold of the sisters, dragging them through the jeering crowd. The sisters struggled to maintain their composure, their hearts pounding as they were pulled toward the local tavern, which had been hastily converted into a makeshift court. The villagers pushed and shoved, driven by a feverish need to see justice done, even if that justice was nothing more than the bloodthirsty wrath of a mob.

The tavern, usually a place of warmth and camaraderie, was now transformed into a dark and foreboding chamber. The tables and chairs had been pushed aside, creating a space for the sisters to stand before the villagers who had gathered to witness their judgment. Once a symbol of comfort, the hearth now cast long, flickering shadows across the room, adding to the atmosphere of dread.

Sir Edward Grantham stood at the head of the room, his hawk-like features sharp and unforgiving in the dim light. Behind him, Matthew Hopkins and John Stearne stood as silent sentinels, their eyes cold and unyielding, eager to see their grim work carried out.

The *Malleus Maleficarum* lay open on a table before him, its pages a grim reminder of the fate that awaited the sisters. The book was large and heavy, its cover worn with age and its pages yellowed.

It was a text that had been used for decades to identify and persecute those accused of witchcraft, a manual of fear and superstition masquerading as law.

Sir Edward held the book aloft for all to see, his voice carrying over the crowd as he spoke. "This is the *Malleus Maleficarum*, a tool of the Church and the law, used to root out the evil of witchcraft wherever it may hide. We will use its guidance to determine the truth of these rumours and bring justice to those who would harm this village."

The crowd murmured again, their fear growing as the book's significance became apparent. The *Malleus Maleficarum* was a weapon, one that had been used to justify countless executions across Europe. In Blackthorn Hollow, its presence here signalled the beginning of something terrible.

Sir Edward returned the book to John Stearne, who opened it and began to read aloud, his voice steady and emotionless.

Eliza scanned the room, her gaze meeting that of several villagers who had once come to them for help, for healing. Those same people looked at her with distrust, their eyes narrowed with suspicion. It was like a veil had been pulled over the village, transforming familiar faces into strangers.

"The marks of a witch are many," Stearne intoned, "but chief among them are these: the ability to harm others through supernatural means, the possession of knowledge forbidden by God, and the use of potions or charms to bring about illness or death."

As Stearne read, the villagers listened in rapt attention, their expressions growing more fearful with each word. The accusations were vague, broad enough to encompass almost anyone who did not fit within the narrow confines of what was considered acceptable by the Church and the law.

Stearne continued, his voice growing more authoritative. "Those accused of witchcraft may be identified by the testimony of witnesses, by the discovery of incriminating items in their possession, or by the presence of unnatural marks on their bodies—signs of a pact with the Devil."

AT THIS, THE VILLAGERS began to shift uneasily, glancing around at one another as if trying to recall if they had seen anything unusual in their neighbours. The fear was palpable, a thick, oppressive weight that seemed to hang over the square like a storm cloud.

Eliza felt her heart race as she listened, her mind racing to think of a way to protect herself and her sisters. She knew the villagers well—knew that most of them were good, decent people who had once trusted the Blackthorn sisters to heal their ailments and ease their suffering. But fear was powerful, and it could turn even the most rational mind against reason.

"We've done nothing wrong," Eliza said firmly, approaching the crowd. "We've only ever used our knowledge to help, to heal. The illness that has struck the village is not of our doing."

Sir Edward's expression was unreadable as he turned to face the sisters. "The words of a witch are lies by their very nature," he said coldly. "You claim to be healers, yet the evidence suggests otherwise. Crops have failed, children have died, and you stand here, denying your role in these tragedies."

Margaret stepped forward, her voice calm but filled with quiet resolve. "We are not witches. We have no power to curse or to harm. Our only power is that of knowledge—knowledge of the earth, of herbs and remedies that can heal."

Sir Edward's eyes narrowed as he regarded Margaret. "And yet, your help seems to have brought nothing but misfortune. The villagers speak of strange occurrences, seeing you consorting with spirits and hearing chants at night. These are the signs of witchcraft, of a pact with the Devil."

"It comes from our ancestors," Margaret replied, her voice unwavering. "It has been passed down through generations of women who understood the natural world and sought to use that understanding for good."

But the villagers were not listening. The fear festering for weeks had now found a target, and the seeds of doubt and suspicion had taken root. Sir

Edward's presence and the *Malleus Maleficarum* in his hand had justified them to act on that fear.

"You claim to heal," one man called out from the crowd, his voice filled with anger, "but my son fell ill after you gave him your so-called remedy. He's dead now. You say you help, but you bring only death!"

Others in the crowd began to shout in agreement, their voices growing louder, more frenzied. The atmosphere in the tavern turned volatile, the villagers' anger bubbling over as they hurled accusations at the sisters.

Eliza felt a wave of despair wash over her. She had known that the tide of fear was turning against them, but she had not realised how quickly it would escalate. The village that had once relied on them for healing had now turned into a mob driven by fear and the promise of retribution.

Sir Edward raised his hand once more, silencing the villagers. "The law is clear," he said, his voice heavy with finality. "Those who practice witchcraft must be brought to justice. The evidence against you is damning, and the people of Blackthorn Hollow demand retribution for the suffering you have caused."

Eliza's heart pounded in her chest. She knew what those "inquiries" meant—interrogation, torture, anything that would force a confession, whether true or false. The *Malleus Maleficarum* outlined such methods in brutal detail, and she knew that once the sisters were taken, their fate was all but sealed.

He turned to his men, who stood ready to carry out his orders. "Take them to the cells," he commanded. "They will remain there until we have gathered more evidence. We will continue the inquiry tomorrow, and if their guilt is confirmed, they will face the punishment prescribed by law."

The sisters were seized by the men, their hands still bound as they were dragged from the tavern. The crowd erupted into a cacophony of cheers and shouts, their bloodlust barely contained. Eliza, Margaret, and Anne exchanged a final, desperate glance as they were pulled toward the door, their fate seemingly sealed.

The sisters exchanged a brief, determined glance before facing the crowd. They would not run; they would not hide. They would face whatever came next with the dignity and strength passed down through generations of Blackthorn women.

As they were led away by Sir Edward and his men, the villagers watched in tense silence. The sisters could feel the weight of their stares, the fear and hatred that had turned them from healers into enemies in the eyes of those they had once helped.

But as they walked through the village they had called home, the sisters held their heads high. They knew the truth and would hold on to it, no matter what came next. They would endure, as they always had.

As they passed through the village square, Eliza caught sight of a figure standing at the edge of the crowd—a young woman with wide, fearful eyes clutching a small child to her chest. Mrs. Turner, Beatrice's mother, had once come to the sisters for help when her daughter was ill.

Their eyes met briefly, and Eliza saw the conflict in the woman's gaze—fear of the unknown and a flicker of doubt and guilt. But the moment passed, Mrs Turner turned away, her face pale and drawn.

The sky above was growing darker, the storm clouds gathering as if responding to the darkness that had descended upon Blackthorn Hollow.

As they were led toward the cells, the cold stone walls of the village's jail looming before them, Eliza could only hope that somehow, some way, they would find a way to survive the storm that was about to descend upon them.

The hammer of witches had fallen, and the sisters knew that nothing would ever be the same again.

Chapter Eight: Uncovering the Past

Emily Ward woke with a start, her heart pounding in her chest. She lay still for a moment, staring up at the ceiling, trying to make sense of the fragments of images that flitted through her mind. The sisters—the Blackthorn sisters—had been there, their ghostly forms almost palpable in the darkness of the attic. She remembered their cold touch, sorrowful eyes, and the overwhelming feeling of injustice filling the room. But now, in the clear morning light, it was hard to tell if it had been real or just a vivid, unsettling dream.

She sat up slowly, rubbing her temples as she tried to shake off the remnants of the night. The journal lay on the nightstand beside her; its worn leather cover reminded her of the events she had witnessed—or imagined. As she reached for it, her fingers hesitated, a shiver running down her spine at the thought of what she might find within its pages.

Had she encountered the spirits of the Blackthorn sisters, or had her mind conjured up the visions after days of intense research and the eerie atmosphere of the cottage? Emily couldn't be sure, but one thing was certain: she couldn't ignore the pull she felt toward their story. She was determined to uncover the truth, whether it was a dream or more.

Pushing the unease aside, Emily dressed and headed to the kitchen to prepare a quick breakfast. The cottage was almost too quiet, and she glanced over her shoulder more than once, half-expecting to see one of the sisters' spectral forms lingering in the shadows. But there was nothing—only the sound of the wind outside and the occasional creak of the old floorboards.

As she sat down with her coffee, Emily resolved to return to the village library. She needed more context to understand the history of Blackthorn Hollow and the fate of the Blackthorn sisters. The journal had provided a glimpse into their lives, but there were still too many unanswered questions.

Mrs. Fletcher, the village librarian, could help her find the missing pieces of the puzzle.

After breakfast, Emily grabbed her coat and the journal and set out for the library. The day was cold and overcast, with a thick blanket of clouds hanging low in the sky. The village was quiet, and the few people she passed on the streets offered polite nods but little more. Emily noticed that some villagers seemed to avoid her gaze, their expressions guarded. It was as if word of her research had already spread, and they were wary of what she might uncover.

When she arrived at the library, she was greeted by the familiar scent of old books and polished wood. The room's warmth was a welcome contrast to the chill outside, and Mrs Fletcher was at her usual spot behind the front desk, sorting through a stack of books. She looked up and smiled as Emily approached.

"Good morning, Dr. Ward," Mrs. Fletcher said warmly. "Back for more research, I see?"

"Good morning, Mrs. Fletcher," Emily replied, returning the smile. "Yes, I hope to learn more about the village's history and the Blackthorn sisters. I found something last night that I think might be important."

Mrs. Fletcher's eyes twinkled with curiosity. "Well, you're in luck. I've been digging through the archives, and I found some additional files that might be of interest to you. There's quite a bit of history here—more than I realised."

She led Emily to a small table near the back of the library, where several old files and documents were laid out. Among them was a large, faded map carefully preserved under a protective plastic layer. Emily's heart skipped a beat as she recognised the village's layout, though it looked very different from how it appeared today.

"This map dates back to the late 16th century," Mrs Fletcher explained, pointing to the various sections of the map. "It shows the village as it was when the Blackthorn sisters lived here. You can see how much has changed over the years—streets have been added, buildings have been demolished, and some areas have been completely built over."

Emily leaned in, studying the map closely. The village was smaller more rural, with large expanses of fields and woodlands surrounding it. Her eyes were drawn to a section of land just outside the village centre, marked with a small cluster of trees.

"These here," Mrs. Fletcher continued, "are the blackthorn trees. The Thornton family owned the land they stood on, which was known for being rich in medicinal plants. The sisters, whose surname has been lost to history, were later called the Blackthorn Sisters because of the blackthorn trees that grew on their land. They likely gathered many of their herbs from these fields."

Emily traced the outline of the trees with her finger, her mind racing. The blackthorn trees had been a vital resource for the sisters, providing the ingredients for their remedies and healing practices. But what had become of the land since then? Had it been preserved, or had it been lost to time?

"Are any of these trees still standing?" Emily asked, her voice tinged with anticipation.

Mrs. Fletcher nodded, though her expression was tinged with sadness. "A few remain, but most were cleared to make way for development. The area has changed significantly over the centuries. What was once open land is now a mixture of homes and streets. Interestingly, some of the streets bear the name of Sir Edward Grantham, the magistrate who led the trial against the sisters."

Emily's heart sank at the thought of the land being lost, but the mention of Sir Edward's name caught her attention. She knew from the journal and her previous research that Sir Edward had played a key role in the sisters' persecution. But the fact that streets had been named after him suggested that his influence had endured long after the trial. What kind of legacy had he left behind, and why had the village chosen to honour him in such a way?

"Why would they name streets after Sir Edward Grantham?" Emily asked, her brow furrowing in confusion. "He was responsible for the sisters' deaths. It seems strange to commemorate him like that."

Mrs. Fletcher sighed, her expression thoughtful. "History is often written by those in power, Dr. Ward. Sir Edward was a prominent figure in the region, and after the trial, he became even more influential. His family continued to hold significant sway in the village for generations, and they were responsible for much of the development that took place. It's possible that the street names were a way to solidify his legacy, to remind the villagers of the authority he wielded."

Emily nodded, the pieces beginning to fall into place. Sir Edward had not only orchestrated the trial but ensured that his name would be remembered and his influence would be felt long after his death. On the other hand, the

Blackthorn sisters had been nearly forgotten, their names erased from history as their land was taken from them.

Determined to learn more, Emily spent the next few hours poring over the documents Mrs Fletcher had provided. Among the files were old property records, letters, and court documents that detailed the events leading up to the sisters' trial. As she read, a clearer picture emerged—one of greed, power, and the systematic erasure of the sisters' legacy.

One document, in particular, caught her eye. It was a land deed, dated shortly after the sisters' execution, transferring ownership of the Blackthorn land to Sir Edward Grantham. The details were vague, but it was clear that the land had been acquired for a fraction of its worth under suspicious circumstances.

Emily's heart raced as she realised the full extent of what had happened. Sir Edward had used the witch trial as a means to seize the Blackthorn land, which was rich in a rare herb needed for a lucrative medicinal treatment. The sisters, far from being malevolent witches, had been victims of a patriarchal society that feared and punished strong, independent women. Their knowledge and skill had made them targets, and Sir Edward had exploited that fear to gain control of their land.

With this new information, Emily knew she needed to see the land for herself. She thanked Mrs Fletcher for her help and set out for the area marked on the map, the fields where the blackthorn trees had once stood. As she walked through the village, she couldn't help but notice the street signs bearing Sir Edward's name, a stark reminder of the injustice that had been done.

When Emily arrived at the site, she found that much of the land had been developed. Houses and streets now occupied what had once been open fields, and the blackthorn trees were reduced to a few solitary survivors. The remaining trees were gnarled and ancient, their branches twisted and barren in the winter cold. They stood like silent sentinels, bearing witness to a history that had been all but forgotten.

Emily walked among the trees, her thoughts heavy with the uncovered knowledge. The air was thick with the scent of damp earth and decaying leaves, and she could almost imagine the sisters moving through these fields, gathering the herbs they would later use to heal the villagers. But now, the land was quiet, the vitality that had once pulsed through it diminished by time and neglect.

As she stood beneath the blackthorn trees, Emily felt a deep sense of loss—not just for the land, but for the sisters who had been wronged. The legacy of Sir Edward Grantham had been preserved, while the true story of the Blackthorn sisters had been buried, their names nearly erased from history.

But Emily was determined to change that. She would bring the truth to light, expose the crimes committed, and restore the sisters' rightful place in history.

As Emily returned to the cottage, the brisk winter air nipping at her cheeks, she noticed a car parked outside. Confusion swept over her—she wasn't expecting any visitors. But as she drew closer, the driver's door opened, and a familiar figure stepped out.

It was James.

A smile broke across Emily's face as she hurried to meet him, her heart lifting at the sight of him. "James! What are you doing here?" she called out, her voice filled with surprise and joy.

James grinned, his eyes warm and affectionate as he approached her. "I managed to get a few days off from the hospital and thought I'd surprise you," he said, pulling her into a hug. "I couldn't wait any longer to see you."

Emily hugged him tightly, the comfort of his presence washing over her like a balm. "I'm so glad you're here," she murmured. "I have so much to tell you."

They walked into the cottage together, the warmth of the fire greeting them as they stepped inside. Emily quickly made tea, eager to share her discoveries with James. Once they were settled on the sofa, cups of steaming tea in hand, she began recounting everything she had learned about the Thornton sisters and their tragic story.

James listened intently, his expression growing more serious as Emily detailed the sisters' work as healers and the circumstances that led to their persecution. James leaned forward when she mentioned the blackthorn trees and the medicinal herbs that once grew on the Thornton land, his interest piqued.

"Their knowledge of herbs and natural remedies would have been extensive," James said thoughtfully, his mind racing through the possibilities. "Back then, people relied heavily on herbal medicine, especially in rural areas with limited access to trained physicians. The sisters would have been well-versed in the properties of various plants and how to use them for healing."

Emily nodded, eager to hear more. "What kind of herbs do you think they would have grown? And what would they have been used for?"

James sipped his tea, his brow furrowing slightly as he considered the question. "Given the era and their role as healers, they would have likely used a wide range of plants. Blackthorn itself was often used to treat digestive issues or sore throats, and it was made into tea from the berries and flowers. But there's more. Yarrow, for example, was commonly used to staunch bleeding and promote wound healing. Comfrey, also known as 'knitbone,' was believed to aid in healing broken bones and bruises—a vital remedy when medical care was rudimentary at best."

He paused, his eyes narrowing in thought. "Then there's valerian, which was used to calm nerves and aid sleep—important in an age when anxiety and insomnia were often linked to spiritual or supernatural causes. St. John's Wort was another key herb known for treating melancholy, which we'd now call depression."

James set down his cup, his expression growing more serious. "But here's the thing: while these remedies were incredibly valuable, the professional medical community of the time was a mixed bag of trained physicians and, frankly, charlatans. Many doctors of the 17th and 18th centuries relied on more harmful than helpful treatments—bloodletting, purging, and the use of toxic substances like mercury were common. These treatments were expensive and often dangerous, which meant that only the wealthy could afford to 'benefit' from them."

Emily listened intently, absorbing the weight of what James was saying. "So, the sisters were offering a safer alternative, but they were doing it for free, or at least for much less than the doctors were charging?"

"Exactly," James replied, his tone grim. "And that made them a threat. The physicians, who were often aligned with the local authorities, saw their incomes and authority diminished by these women who provided effective treatments without the cost. It's not hard to imagine that some of these doctors were keen to get rid of the competition, especially if they could do so under the guise of eradicating witchcraft."

He leaned back, his expression thoughtful. "In fact, during this period, accusations of witchcraft were often rooted in economic and social tensions. Women who were knowledgeable in herbal remedies were easy targets. The

Malleus Maleficarum, the infamous witch-hunting manual, actually encouraged the persecution of women who were seen as healers or midwives, branding their practices as witchcraft."

Emily's eyes widened as James continued. "The Thornton sisters were caught in a perfect storm in many ways. They were skilled, independent women in a time when such qualities were seen as threatening. And they provided a valuable service that undermined the local physicians, who likely viewed them as both a nuisance and a danger."

The pieces were falling into place for Emily. "And that's where Sir Edward Grantham comes in. He used the fear of witchcraft to eliminate them, seize their land, and remove the threat they posed to the local physicians—and to his own power and influence."

James nodded, his expression darkening slightly. "It all fits. The sisters were convenient scapegoats, and their land—rich in valuable herbs—was the prize. Sir Edward likely saw the trial as a way to kill two birds with one stone: consolidate his power and remove the competition."

Emily felt a surge of determination. "I have to keep going. There's more to this story; I can feel it. And I won't stop until I've brought it all to light."

James reached over and took her hand, giving it a reassuring squeeze. "You're getting closer to the truth, Emily. Everything you've found so far points to a deliberate effort to erase the sisters and their legacy. But you're uncovering it, piece by piece."

Emily sat in the cosy warmth of the cottage, the shadows of the past closing in around her. As she absorbed everything James had shared, her resolve only strengthened. The Thornton sisters' story was one of tragedy but also one of resilience—and Emily was determined to ensure their voices were finally heard.

James's insights had provided valuable context, and Emily was already planning her next steps. The puzzle pieces were coming together, and she felt more driven than ever to uncover the full truth. The story of the Thornton sisters wasn't just an academic pursuit—it was a mission to restore justice, and Emily was ready to face whatever challenges lay ahead with unwavering determination.

She glanced at James, appreciating his support but knowing that this was her journey. The Thornton sisters had been silenced for too long, and Emily's voice would break that silence.

Chapter Nine: The Trial Begins

The winter sun hung low in the sky, casting long, ominous shadows over Blackthorn Hollow as the villagers gathered in the square. A hush fell over the crowd, their breath visible in the cold air, as the Thornton sisters were led into the heart of the village, their hands bound and their heads held high. Despite the fear that clutched at their hearts, Eliza, Margaret, and Anne walked with dignity, refusing to bow to the terror that had consumed the village.

The once-bustling village square, where markets and festivals had taken place, was now a grim prelude to the horror unfolding inside the old tavern. The building, which had once been a place of warmth and community, now stood dark and foreboding, its wooden beams creaking under the weight of the unspeakable acts about to take place within. The villagers filed inside, their faces pale with fear and anticipation, as the sisters were dragged toward the tavern's entrance.

Inside, the air was thick with the scent of damp wood and spilled ale, the warmth of the hearth doing little to dispel the coldness that seemed to seep into the very walls. The tables and chairs had been pushed aside, creating a space for the sisters to stand before the crowd. The flickering candlelight cast long shadows across the room, adding to the oppressive atmosphere.

At the head of the room stood Sir Edward Grantham, a powerful and malevolent figure who had manipulated the village's fear for his own gain. His eyes gleamed with satisfaction as he watched the sisters being brought before the villagers. The old tavern, once a place of merriment and laughter, had been transformed into a chamber of dread where justice would be twisted to serve the whims of the powerful.

The sisters had been formally accused of witchcraft, and the village had been whipped into a frenzy by Sir Edward and the infamous Witchfinder General, Matthew Hopkins. Hopkins, along with his associate John Stearne, had become notorious across the region for his relentless pursuit of so-called witches, and he had now turned his attention to Blackthorn Hollow.

Sir Edward began to speak as the sisters stood before the crowd, his voice cold and authoritative. "People of Blackthorn Hollow," he called out, "we are here to bring justice to our village. The Thornton sisters stand accused of witchcraft, of consorting with the Devil, and of bringing curses upon our land. The evidence against them is overwhelming."

A murmur of agreement rippled through the crowd, the fear in the air palpable. Sir Edward gestured to Hopkins and Stearne, who stepped forward with grim expressions. These men had made a name for themselves by accusing women and the poor of witchcraft, and they were paid handsomely for every so-called witch they brought to trial.

Hopkins unfurled a scroll, his voice dripping with condescension as he read the charges against the sisters. "Eliza Thornton, Margaret Thornton, Anne Thornton—you stand accused of attending Holy Communion with a familiar, demonic cat named Grimalkin, who serves as your agent in this world. You are further accused of having visions of the Devil and his demons and of using your familiars to harm your neighbours."

The crowd gasped, their fear deepening as Hopkins continued. "It has been testified that you, Eliza Thornton, claimed to commune with this familiar only to inquire about the health of those who came to you for healing. Yet we know that such communion is not with God but with the Devil himself!"

Eliza stepped forward, her voice calm but firm as she addressed the crowd. "I have only ever sought to help those in need," she said, her gaze steady. "The cat Grimalkin is no demon but a creature of God's creation. I asked him only for guidance in healing the sick, nothing more."

But her words were drowned out by the jeers and shouts of the villagers. The seeds of doubt and fear that had been planted by Sir Edward and Hopkins had taken root, and there was no room for reason or truth in the crowd's minds.

Margaret was next to be accused. "Margaret Thornton," Hopkins intoned, "you are accused of consorting with familiar spirits, of using these demons to bring death upon your neighbours, and of meeting in secret with your sisters to perform unholy rites."

Margaret lifted her chin, her hazel eyes filled with quiet defiance. "The visions I have seen are not of the Devil, but of the suffering of those around me. I have never harmed another soul—only sought to bring comfort and healing."

But her words, too, fell on deaf ears. The villagers were too far gone, their minds poisoned by the hysteria that had swept through the village.

Anne was accused last. Hopkins' voice grew even more ominous as he read out the charges. "Anne Thornton, you are accused of meeting in secret with your sisters, of reading from mysterious books filled with forbidden knowledge, and of using your power to kill those who have crossed you."

Anne's green eyes flashed with anger as she responded. "I have read no forbidden books, and I have killed no one. The knowledge I possess is that which was passed down through generations—knowledge of healing, not harm."

The crowd's reaction was swift and brutal. The accusations, though baseless, were more than enough to condemn the sisters in the eyes of the villagers. Seeing that the crowd was firmly on his side, Sir Edward pressed forward with the trial.

FINALLY, SIR EDWARD addressed the local magistrate, a man easily swayed by the Witchfinder General's influence. "The evidence is clear," Sir Edward declared. "The Thornton sisters are guilty of witchcraft. Their communion with demonic familiars, their visions of the Devil, and their secret meetings to practise dark magic all confirm this."

The magistrate, pale and trembling, nodded in agreement. "The Thornton sisters," he pronounced, "are at this moment found guilty of witchcraft. They shall be held in the dungeons of Colchester Castle until their final punishment is determined."

The sisters were led away in chains, their heads held high despite the horror of what had just transpired. The villagers, once their friends and neighbours, had turned against them, driven by fear and the manipulations of Sir Edward and the Witchfinder General.

As they were taken from Blackthorn Hollow, the sisters could only hope the truth would be revealed. But for now, they were to be imprisoned in the dark, dank dungeons of Colchester Castle, where many accused witches before them had languished and died.

The wind howled through the ancient stone walls of Colchester Castle, a mournful wail that echoed through the narrow corridors and seeped into the dark recesses of the dungeons below. The Thornton sisters, Eliza, Margaret, and Anne, were dragged through the castle's heavy wooden doors, their chains clinking with each reluctant step. The cold stone beneath their feet and the damp, musty air that filled their lungs were just the beginning of the torment that awaited them.

Once a proud symbol of Norman power, the castle had fallen into disrepair over the centuries. Its crumbling walls and drafty halls now served a darker purpose—where the accused, the feared, and the forgotten were sent to await their fate. For the Thornton sisters, this ancient fortress would be their prison and, possibly, their tomb.

The gaoler, a cruel, sallow-faced man with a permanent sneer, greeted them with a leer as they were thrust into the dungeon. His eyes glinted with sadistic pleasure as he surveyed the new arrivals, his hands twitching with anticipation of the power he would wield over them.

"Welcome to your new home, witches," he spat, his voice thick with contempt. "You'll find it's not as hospitable as your little village."

The sisters said nothing, their faces pale but defiant as they were forced into one of the dank cells. The iron door creaked shut behind them, and the gaoler turned the key with a sense of finality that echoed through the stone chamber. The cell was small and claustrophobic, with only a tiny barred window high above that allowed in a sliver of pale daylight. The stone walls were cold and slick with moisture, and the floor was littered with damp and mouldy straw. The air was thick with the stench of rot and decay, mingling with the scent of fear that seemed to cling to the very stones.

Eliza, Margaret, and Anne huddled together on the filthy straw, their bodies trembling from the cold and the weight of their chains. The cell offered little protection from the elements; the wind howled through the cracks in the walls, bringing a chill that cut to the bone. The cold was unbearable at night, and the sisters' breath was visible in the frigid air as they huddled together for warmth. The dampness seeped into their clothes and skin, and they could feel the numbness creeping into their limbs.

The gaoler, who took sadistic pleasure in his duties, would occasionally pass by their cell to taunt them, his eyes gleaming with malice. "A few more days in here, and you'll confess to anything," he would sneer, his voice dripping with disdain. "Even if you didn't start out as witches, you'll believe you are before long."

But the worst was not the cold or the taunts but the gnawing fear of what was to come. They knew well the reputation of the man who had imprisoned them—Matthew Hopkins, the self-proclaimed Witchfinder General, who had made a name for himself by rooting out witches and bringing them to trial. Hopkins was relentless in his pursuit, driven by a fanatical belief in the existence of witchcraft and a lust for the power that came with his position.

Hopkins was the son of a rector, and his zeal was born from a twisted sense of righteousness. He claimed to be doing God's work by hunting down women who, he believed, consorted with the Devil to bring misfortune upon their communities. His methods were as cruel as they were effective. He was paid for every witch he found every confession he extracted, and he had become notorious for his brutal techniques.

The sisters had heard the stories—how Hopkins would deprive his victims of sleep, keeping them awake for days on end until their minds broke under the strain. How he would strip them of their clothes and prick their skin with needles, searching for spots that did not bleed, which he claimed were the Devil's marks. And how he would throw them into the water, the so-called "trial by water," where the innocent would sink, and the guilty would float—a twisted logic that condemned the innocent as easily as the guilty.

The sisters knew that they would soon face these horrors themselves. They had no illusions about the fairness of their trial or the likelihood of escaping with their lives. The Witchfinder General had made up his mind, and once Hopkins set his sights on a victim, there was little hope of reprieve.

The interrogations began almost immediately. The sisters were dragged from their cell, one by one, and taken to a dark chamber deep within the castle. There, they were confronted by Matthew Hopkins himself, his thin lips curled into a cruel smile as he surveyed his captives. His eyes were cold and calculating, devoid of any compassion or mercy.

"You know why you're here," Hopkins said, his voice low and menacing. "You've been accused of witchcraft, of consorting with the Devil and bringing ruin upon your village. Confess now, and perhaps your suffering will be lessened."

Eliza met his gaze with a steely determination. "We have nothing to confess," she replied, her voice steady despite the fear that gripped her. "We are not witches. We have harmed no one."

Hopkins' smile widened, his eyes narrowing with sadistic pleasure. "That's what they all say," he murmured, almost to himself. "But we have ways of finding the truth."

The torture began in earnest. Hopkins and his men subjected the sisters to all manner of horrors. They were kept awake for days, their eyes forced open with slivers of wood, their bodies wracked with exhaustion and pain. The lack of sleep soon took its toll, their minds beginning to fray as the hours dragged on.

Margaret, the most spiritual of the three, tried to focus on her prayers, but even her faith began to falter as the torture continued. She was stripped of her clothes and pricked with needles, the men searching her body for any sign of a mark, any blemish that could be interpreted as a sign of the Devil's touch. Her skin, already pale from the cold, was soon marred with tiny wounds, each one a testament to her suffering.

Anne fought against the men as they tried to drag her to the water pit. But her strength was no match for their numbers, and she was soon plunged into the icy depths. The water was bitterly cold, seeping into her bones as she struggled to stay afloat. The villagers watched in silence, their fear of witchcraft so deep that they were willing to believe that even this innocent girl could be in league with the Devil.

Eliza was spared none of these horrors. She endured the same sleep deprivation, the same pricking and prodding, her body and mind pushed to their limits. But through it all, she refused to give Hopkins the satisfaction of a confession. She knew that to admit to witchcraft would be to condemn them all, to provide the Witchfinder with the evidence he needed to justify their execution.

Days turned into weeks, and still, the sisters endured. They were returned to their cell after each interrogation, their bodies broken and bruised but their spirits unyielding. The gaoler would leer at them as they were thrown back into the darkness, his cruel laughter echoing in the small chamber.

"You'll confess soon enough," he would say, his voice filled with a sickening glee. "They all do, in the end."

But the sisters remained resolute. They clung to each other for strength, their bond growing stronger as their bodies weakened. They whispered words of comfort and encouragement in the dark, promising each other that they would not break, that they would not give in to the fear and pain that sought to consume them.

Yet, deep down, they knew that their time was running out. The Witchfinder General was not a man who accepted defiance easily. He would continue to torture them, to wear them down until they had no choice but to confess—or until they died from the strain.

The cold, the darkness, the endless torment—it was all designed to break them, to strip away their humanity and reduce them to nothing more than frightened, desperate creatures willing to say anything to make the pain stop. And still, they held on.

But even the strongest of wills can only endure so much. One night, after a particularly brutal session, Margaret collapsed onto the floor of their cell, her body trembling uncontrollably. The cold had seeped so deeply into her bones that she could no longer feel her fingers or toes, and the pain from her wounds had become a constant, throbbing agony.

"I can't..." she whispered, her voice weak and broken. "I can't do this anymore."

Eliza and Anne huddled close to her, their bodies shaking with cold and exhaustion. "We have to hold on," Eliza murmured, her voice as firm as she could. "We have to stay strong for each other."

But even as she spoke, she could feel her own resolve beginning to waver. How much longer could they endure this? How much longer before they broke, before they gave Hopkins the confession he so desperately wanted?

In the darkness of their cell, the sisters clung to each other, their faith and hope slipping away with each passing day. The walls of Colchester Castle seemed to close in around them, the weight of centuries of suffering pressing down on their souls.

And still, the wind howled outside a mournful dirge that cchocd through the ancient stones—a reminder that, for the Thornton sisters, there would be no escape from the darkness that had claimed them.

Chapter Ten: Emily's Search for the Truth

Emily Ward sat at the oak table in the kitchen, her laptop open before her, surrounded by a sea of documents and old records. The fire in the hearth behind her crackled gently, its warmth a welcome reprieve from the chill that clung to the air. Despite the comfort of the room, a cold unease had settled in Emily's chest, a feeling that had grown stronger with every new piece of information she uncovered.

James was busy making tea in the adjoining kitchen, his presence a comforting backdrop as Emily delved deeper into the history of the Thornton sisters. He had offered to help her with her research, but for the moment, he was content to keep her company, sensing that she needed to process her findings alone.

Emily had spent hours poring over the papers, piecing together the fragments of history that had long been buried. The further she dug, the more she was convinced that the Thornton sisters had been wrongfully accused. The tale of witchcraft and curses that had been woven around them was a fabrication—a tool used by powerful men to seize what they wanted.

She glanced up as James placed a steaming mug of tea beside her.

"Thanks," she murmured, her fingers brushing the handle as she continued to scroll through the digitised court records on her laptop.

James leaned against the counter, sipping his tea. "How's it going? Found anything new?"

Emily nodded, though her expression remained serious. "I think I've found something that could prove the sisters were innocent—at least prove they were set up."

James raised an eyebrow, his interest piqued. "Really? What have you got?"

Emily reached for a folder on the table, pulling out a few sheets of yellow paper. "It's a series of letters between Sir Edward Grantham and another magistrate. They're written in the usual formal language, but there's something sinister about how he talks about the trial. He's practically gloating."

James frowned as he took one of the letters from her, scanning the text. "He was pleased with the outcome?"

"Yes," Emily replied, her voice hardening. "He was delighted. And I think it's because he knew that once the sisters were out of the way, he'd gain control of their land—known for its medicinal herbs. That land was valuable, and I think he would do whatever it took to get it."

James set the letter down, his face serious. "That's quite the accusation, Emily. Do you think you'll be able to prove it?"

"I'm not sure," Emily admitted, her shoulders sagging slightly. "But I have to try. The more I uncover, the more convinced I am that this was all about power and greed. Sir Edward needed a scapegoat, and the sisters were perfect for the role—especially with someone like Matthew Hopkins involved."

James let out a low whistle. "The Witchfinder General himself. It's no wonder the sisters didn't stand a chance. Hopkins was infamous for his witch hunts. He practically created a business out of accusing women of witchcraft."

Emily nodded grimly. "Exactly. And Sir Edward used Hopkins to legitimise his agenda. They whipped the village into a frenzy between them and ensured that the trial was a foregone conclusion."

She leaned back in her chair, rubbing her temples as the weight of the situation settled over her. "The problem is, bringing this to light isn't easy. The village has held onto its version of events for centuries, and many people won't want to see that narrative challenged."

James placed a reassuring hand on her shoulder. "You're doing the right thing, Emily. If there's even a chance that the sisters were innocent, their story deserves to be told."

Emily looked up at him, grateful for his support. "I know. It's just... I can't shake the feeling that something—or someone—doesn't want this truth to come out. The locals have been polite, but they're getting more distant. Even Mrs Fletcher at the library has started giving me the cold shoulder."

"People are afraid of change," James said gently. "Especially when it comes to something as deeply ingrained as history. But that doesn't mean you should stop."

Emily smiled faintly, taking a sip of her tea. "No, I won't stop. I owe it to the sisters to keep going."

She glanced at the stack of papers on the table, then back at James. "I need to visit some of the locations connected to the trial—the old tavern, the place where the sisters were imprisoned, and the site where they were hanged. It might help me get a clearer picture of what happened."

James nodded, setting his mug down. "I'll come with you. It's not safe for you to go poking around alone, especially if you're stirring up things that people would rather leave buried."

Emily hesitated for a moment, then nodded in agreement. "All right. But be warned—it might get a bit eerie. I've been experiencing... things."

"Things?" James echoed, his tone concerned.

"Strange occurrences. Shadows are moving objects, not where I left them... and the dreams. They're getting more vivid. It's like I'm seeing what the sisters saw, feeling what they felt."

James frowned, his brow furrowed in concern. "Emily, if this is affecting you—"

"I'm fine," she cut in quickly, though she wasn't entirely sure it was true. "I just need to see this through. I think the sisters are trying to tell me something, and I can't ignore that."

James studied her for a moment, then nodded. "All right. But if it gets too much, promise me you'll take a step back."

"I promise," Emily said, though she wasn't sure she could keep that promise. The pull to uncover the truth was too strong.

They finished their tea in silence, the weight of their task pressing down on them both. After clearing the table, they put on their coats and headed into the crisp morning air. The village of Blackthorn Hollow was quiet, and the streets were empty as they made their way to the old tavern.

The building stood at the edge of the village square, its stone walls and timber beams darkened with age. The tavern had been well preserved, a relic of a bygone era, but as Emily and James stepped inside, they could feel the weight of history pressing down on them. The atmosphere was thick with memories, the air heavy with the scent of old wood and lingering fear.

"This is where it started," Emily murmured, eyes scanning the dim interior. "This is where the accusations were made, where the sisters were dragged in front of the villagers and condemned."

James nodded, his gaze sweeping the room. "It's hard to imagine what it must have been like. The fear, the hysteria... the sisters must have known there was no escape."

Emily walked slowly through the tavern, her fingers trailing along the rough wooden tables the worn benches where villagers once sat, whispering accusations and feeding the flames of panic. She could almost hear their voices, see their faces twisted with fear and suspicion.

"This place has seen so much pain," she said quietly, stopping before the large stone fireplace. "But I think it's also where the sisters made their stand. They knew they were innocent and didn't back down, even when everyone turned against them."

James joined her by the fireplace, his expression thoughtful. "It takes incredible strength to do that. Hold on to the truth, even when the whole world tells you you're wrong."

EMILY NODDED, HER EYES distant as she tried to imagine what it must have been like for the sisters in those final days. "They must have been terrified. But they didn't break. And now, I must ensure their story isn't lost."

As she spoke, a figure emerged from the dimly lit corner of the tavern, moving purposefully towards them. The man was tall and broad-shouldered, with a weathered face that suggested he had seen more than his fair share of years. His expression was stern, his brow furrowed as if he were grappling with some inner turmoil. He stopped a few feet away from the table, his piercing blue eyes fixed on Emily.

"Are you Dr Ward?" he asked, his voice rough and laden with a barely concealed edge of irritation.

Emily looked up, startled by the interruption. "Yes, I am," she replied, her tone measured and polite. "Can I help you with something?"

The man's jaw tightened, and he stepped closer, his gaze flickering to James before returning to Emily. "I've heard you're investigating the Thornton sisters," he said, his voice low but firm. "Digging up things that are better left buried."

Emily exchanged a quick glance with James, who was already sitting up a little straighter, his eyes narrowing as he assessed the situation. "I am looking into the history of the Thornton sisters, yes," Emily confirmed, keeping her voice calm. "I believe their story deserves to be told."

The man's frown deepened, and he shook his head slowly. "You should leave it alone, Dr Ward. Some things are best left in the past."

Something in his tone made Emily's stomach churn with unease. "I'm sorry," she replied carefully, "but I can't do that. The truth needs to come out."

The man's eyes darkened, and his voice was harsher. "I'm telling you, you don't know what you're getting yourself into. This village has its secrets, which are not for you to uncover."

James, who had been quietly watching the exchange, suddenly leaned forward, his gaze fixed on the man. "Is that a threat?" he asked, his voice steady but carrying an unmistakable undertone of warning.

The man's lips pressed into a thin line, and for a moment, it seemed he was weighing his options. He held James's gaze, and a tense silence settled over the table. Then, without another word, he turned and walked away, disappearing back into the shadows from where he had emerged.

Emily watched him go, her heart pounding in her chest. She couldn't shake the feeling that the man knew more than he was letting on—that he was somehow connected to the dark history she was trying to uncover.

"Well, that was unsettling," James muttered, his eyes still trained on where the man had disappeared.

Emily nodded, her thoughts racing. "He's hiding something," she said quietly. "And whatever it is, it's linked to the Thornton sisters. I'm sure of it."

James looked at her, his expression serious. "Do you think he's connected to Sir Edward Grantham?"

"I don't know," Emily admitted, "but I intend to find out."

As they sat in the quiet tavern, the weight of the encounter hung heavily between them. The man's warning had only strengthened Emily's resolve. She was determined to uncover whatever secrets Blackthorn Hollow was hiding—even if it meant facing threats from those who wanted the past to stay buried.

Emily couldn't shake the uneasy feeling that she had just brushed up against something far more dangerous than anticipated. The man's words echoed in her mind: "Some things are best left in the past."

They left the tavern in a sombre mood, the weight of the past heavy on their shoulders. Their next stop was where the sisters had been imprisoned overnight—the old cells, now nothing more than a crumbling ruin at the edge of the village.

The building had been reduced to a pile of rubble, the stones overgrown with ivy and brambles. The wind picked up as Emily and James approached, rustling the leaves and sending a chill down their spines.

"This is where they were held," Emily said, her voice barely above a whisper.

"We need to also go to Colchester Castle," she said, turning to James. Her voice was steady, but there was an urgency behind her words. "That's where they were taken after the trial. Where they were imprisoned and tortured before... before the end."

James met her gaze, understanding the unspoken determination in her eyes. "Colchester Castle," he repeated, nodding in agreement. "If that's where the next piece of the puzzle is, then that's where we'll go."

As they walked away from the ruins, the wind blew through the ivy and brambles as if the past was urging them forward. Emily's heart pounded with a mix of anticipation and dread. Colchester Castle held the final, darkest chapter of the Thornton sisters' story—a place where justice had been twisted into something cruel and monstrous.

She knew that what awaited them there would not be easy to face. But the truth had to be uncovered, and the sisters deserved to have their voices heard, no matter how long it had taken.

"We'll find the answers," Emily murmured, more to herself than to James, as they returned to the car. "And we'll make sure their story isn't forgotten."

James placed a reassuring hand on her shoulder. "We will," he said firmly. "Whatever it takes."

With renewed resolve, they set off towards Colchester, the shadows of Blackthorn Hollow receding behind them as they moved closer to the heart of the mystery. The journey ahead would be challenging, but Emily was ready. The

Thornton sisters had waited long enough for justice, and she was determined to be the one to deliver it.

Colchester Castle loomed before Emily and James as they approached, its ancient stone walls towering above them like a sentinel of history. The fortress had stood for centuries, its thick, weathered stones bearing witness to the darkest moments of England's past. As they crossed the threshold into the castle grounds, Emily felt a sense of foreboding settle over her, as if the very air was heavy with the memories of those who had suffered within these walls.

Inside the castle, they were led down a narrow staircase that spiralled into the depths of the building. The further they descended, the colder and damper the air became, the light from above gradually dimming until they were enveloped in a murky gloom. The walls, slick with moisture, seemed to close in around them, adding to the oppressive atmosphere.

The gaol was a labyrinth of narrow, claustrophobic corridors lined with heavy, rusted iron doors. The cells were small, cramped spaces with barely enough room to stand, let alone lie down. The stone floors were uneven, and a persistent drip of water echoed through the silence, creating an eerie, maddening rhythm.

Emily peered into one of the cells, her breath catching in her throat. The space was dark, the only light coming from a small, barred window high up on the wall. The walls were rough, cold stone, and the smell of damp and decay was overpowering. She could see the remains of what might have been straw on the floor, long since rotted away to a filthy, mouldy heap.

"This is where they were kept," she whispered, her voice trembling slightly. "This is where the Thornton sisters spent their final days."

James stood beside her, his expression grim. "It's barbaric," he muttered, shaking his head. "To keep anyone in conditions like this... it's inhumane."

The gaoler, a surly man with a sallow complexion and a perpetual scowl, watched them from the shadows, his eyes narrowed with suspicion. He had been less than welcoming when they arrived, clearly uncomfortable with their interest in the castle's dark history.

"They say the witches would confess anything just to be freed from these cells," the gaoler said gruffly, his voice echoing off the stone walls. "But it was never enough. They'd be dragged out of here, only to face the noose."

Emily's heart ached as she imagined the sisters, terrified and broken, trapped in this hellish place. The thought of them enduring such conditions—cold, hungry, and tortured—made her all the more determined to see their story brought to light.

"They didn't stand a chance," she murmured, more to herself than to James. "Not with men like Matthew Hopkins and Sir Edward Grantham hunting them down."

James placed a hand on her shoulder, his grip firm and reassuring. "We'll make sure the truth is told, Emily. They deserve that."

Emily nodded, her resolve hardening. She could almost feel the presence of the sisters, their spirits lingering in the cold, dark corners of the gaol, waiting for someone to speak on their behalf finally.

But as they made their way back up the narrow staircase, leaving the stifling darkness of the gaol behind, Emily knew there was still one more place they needed to visit—a place where the Thornton sisters' tragic story had reached its bitter conclusion.

The journey back to Blackthorn Hollow was quiet, the mood sombre as they drove through the winding country roads. The sky was overcast, the clouds hanging low and heavy, casting the landscape in a dull, muted light. Emily's mind was focused on what lay ahead—the final, tragic chapter of the Thornton sisters' story.

WHEN THEY ARRIVED BACK in the village, the sun was beginning to set, casting long shadows across the fields. The villagers were scarce, most having retreated indoors as the evening chill set in. Emily and James parked the car at the edge of the village and set off on foot towards the outskirts, where the site of the hangings was located.

The path took them through a small, overgrown clearing, uneven ground and littered with the remnants of long-forgotten gravestones. In the centre of the clearing stood a single, ancient tree, its gnarled branches twisted and bare. The blackthorn tree had stood there for centuries, its roots deep in the earth that had witnessed so much pain and sorrow.

"This is where they were hanged," Emily said softly, her voice barely above a whisper. "This is where it ended."

The tree loomed over them, its dark, twisted branches reaching out like skeletal fingers. The ground beneath it was barren, the grass sparse and patchy, as if the very earth had rejected the life that had once been there. The wind rustled through the branches, creating a haunting melody that sent a shiver down Emily's spine.

She stood silently momentarily, her heart heavy with grief for the sisters. They had been dragged from their cells, beaten down by weeks of torture and deprivation, only to be brought to this place to meet their end. The villagers, whipped into a frenzy by fear and superstition, had gathered to watch, convinced that they were ridding their village of evil.

Emily reached out, her hand brushing the rough bark of the tree. As her fingers made contact, she was suddenly overwhelmed by a vivid and intense vision that took her breath away. She was no longer in the present but thrust into the past, into the sisters' final moments.

SHE COULD FEEL THE rough rope around her neck, the cold wind biting at her skin, and the weight of despair pressing down on her. She heard the jeers of the crowd, saw their faces twisted with fear and hatred, and felt the unbearable pain as the noose tightened.

The vision released its grip on her as quickly as it had come, leaving her gasping for breath. She stumbled back, her hand clutching her chest as her heart raced.

"Emily!" James caught her as she swayed, his face pale with worry. "Are you all right? What happened?"

Emily nodded shakily, her mind struggling to process what she had just experienced. "I... I saw it, James. I was there in their final moments. I felt everything they felt. It was so real."

James looked at her with deep concern. "This is getting too much for you, Emily. Maybe we should—"

"No." Emily shook her head, her resolve hardening once more. "I'm not giving up now. The sisters are reaching out to me, trying to show me what really happened. I have to finish this. I have to make sure their story is told."

James hesitated, then nodded. "All right. But I'm staying with you every step of the way."

They returned to the cottage as the afternoon light faded, the sky tinged with the soft hues of dusk. Emily's mind was racing with everything she had seen and felt, but she knew the hardest part was still ahead of her.

She sat down at the table, her hands trembling slightly as she began to compile her findings. The letters, the records, the testimonies—every piece of evidence she had gathered pointed to one undeniable truth: Sir Edward Grantham had orchestrated the trial to gain control of the Thornton sisters' land, and Matthew Hopkins had been all too eager to help him.

As she worked, the atmosphere in the cottage seemed to shift. The shadows lengthened, the firelight flickering uneasily on the walls. Objects that had been neatly arranged began to shift on their own, moving ever so slightly as if guided by unseen hands. The air crackled with an almost palpable energy as though the very walls of the cottage were alive with the spirits of the past.

But Emily was no longer afraid. She could feel the sisters' presence, urging her on, pushing her to reveal the truth. Their story had been twisted and buried for centuries, but now, finally, it was coming to light.

James watched her silently, his concern for her evident, but he knew better than to interrupt. He could see the determination in her eyes, and the fire ignited within her.

As the night deepened, Emily's resolve only grew stronger. She would not let the Thornton sisters be forgotten. She would bring their story to the world, no matter the opposition she faced.

As she finished her work, the last pieces of the puzzle falling into place, she felt a sense of peace settle over her. The spirits of the Thornton sisters had found an ally in Emily Ward, and together, they would see justice done.

But the journey was far from over. The truth had been uncovered, but now came the challenge of making the world believe it. Emily knew that some would resist her findings and would fight to keep the old narrative alive. But she also knew that the truth had a power all its own, and with James by her side, she was ready to face whatever came next.

The Thornton sisters had suffered greatly, but they had not been broken. Their strength and resilience had endured through the centuries, and now, through Emily's work, their voices would finally be heard.

As the first light of dawn began to break over the horizon, Emily felt a quiet satisfaction. The path ahead might be difficult, but she was ready. She would see this through to the end, for the sisters and the truth.

And as the spirits of the past finally began to rest, Emily knew that she had found her purpose.

Chapter Eleven: The Curse Unleashed

The damp, cold stone walls of Colchester Castle loomed over the three Blackthorn sisters as they huddled together in their cramped cell. Once a Roman fortress, the castle had been repurposed as a prison, its ancient stones now echoing the cries of those accused of heresy, treason, and witchcraft. Eliza, Margaret, and Anne Blackthorn had been imprisoned here for weeks, their only company the scurrying rats and the guards who spat curses at them whenever they passed.

Eliza sat with her back against the wall, her eyes closed in a futile attempt to block out the misery surrounding them. Margaret whispered prayers under her breath, her fingers tracing the small, crude cross she had carved into the stone. Anne stared out of the small, barred window at the sliver of grey sky visible above, her thoughts far from the horrors of their situation.

In the weeks since their arrest, the sisters had endured relentless questioning, torture, and humiliation. The Witchfinder General, Matthew Hopkins—a man of cold, calculated cruelty—had taken particular pleasure in their suffering, convinced that their confessions would prove his righteousness and authority. But despite the pain and terror inflicted upon them, the sisters had refused to confess to crimes they had not committed.

On this day, however, their fate had been sealed. A guard appeared at the door of their cell, his face devoid of emotion as he announced that they would be transported back to Blackthorn Hollow for their trial. The journey would be their last, for in their hearts, the sisters knew the trial's outcome had already been decided.

The journey back to Blackthorn Hollow was a sombre affair. The sisters were loaded into a wooden cart, their hands bound and their ankles shackled. A contingent of guards, along with Sir Edward Grantham and the Witchfinder General, accompanied them, their expressions stern and unyielding. The villagers of Colchester, having heard of the infamous Blackthorn sisters, gathered along the streets to watch the cart pass by, their faces a mixture of fear, curiosity, and hatred.

The village that had once held them in high esteem, where they had been loved by many, now stood silent. The people who had once sought their help now gazed upon them with cold indifference. Their faces were a conflicted mix of fear and curiosity, with more than a few marked by simmering hatred.

As the cart rumbled over the cobblestone streets, the sisters exchanged glances, their unspoken thoughts reflected in each other's eyes. The bond between them, forged through years of shared experiences and hardships, was unbreakable. They had always stood together in times of joy or sorrow and would face this final trial as one.

The countryside passed in a blur of green and grey as the cart approached Blackthorn Hollow. The sky, heavy with dark clouds, seemed to mirror the weight of the doom that hung over them. The air was thick with the scent of rain and the earthy smell of the fields, but none of the sisters took comfort in the familiar surroundings. They knew that this was no homecoming—this was a return to the place where their lives would end.

As they neared Blackthorn Hollow, the village's thatched roofs and crooked chimneys stood stark against the darkening sky. What had once been a place of warmth and community filled the sisters with dread. The villagers, who had once been their neighbours and friends, had turned against them, manipulated by fear and the machinations of Sir Edward and the Witchfinder General.

The cart halted in the centre of the village, where a crowd had already gathered outside the Tavern, the largest building in Blackthorn Hollow. Without a shred of dignity, the sisters were roughly pulled from the cart by the gaoler and the Witchfinder General. Their chains clinked ominously as they were marched toward the Tavern. The villagers parted to let them pass, their eyes a mix of pity, guilt, and condemnation.

The interior of the Tavern was dimly lit, the smell of stale ale and smoke hanging heavy in the air. The large common room, usually filled with laughter and conversation, was now silent, the air thick with tension. A makeshift courtroom had been set up at the far end of the room, with a long table serving as the bench for the magistrate and the Witchfinder General.

Sir Edward Grantham, resplendent in his magistrate's robes, sat at the head of the table, expressing grim satisfaction. Beside him, Matthew Hopkins, the

Witchfinder General, was a stark contrast, his cold, calculating gaze sweeping over the room, taking in every detail. His presence alone was enough to strike fear into the hearts of those who knew of his ruthless methods.

The sisters were brought before the table, their chains rattling as they were forced to kneel on the hard wooden floor. The room was packed with villagers, their faces illuminated by the flickering light of the torches that lined the walls. The atmosphere was thick with the scent of fear and anticipation as the villagers waited for the trial to begin.

Sir Edward stood, his voice cutting through the silence like a knife. "We are gathered here today to bring justice upon those who have brought darkness and evil into our village. The Blackthorn sisters stand accused of witchcraft, of consorting with the devil, and of using their foul powers to harm the good people of Blackthorn Hollow."

He paused, letting his words sink in, before continuing. "These charges are grave, and the evidence against them is overwhelming. They have been found to possess charms, potions, and books of dark magic. Witnesses have come forward to testify to their unnatural practices, their ability to cure the incurable, and their manipulation of the elements."

The Witchfinder General, his face devoid of emotion, spoke next. "The evidence has been thoroughly examined, and it is clear that these women are guilty of the crimes for which they stand accused. Their knowledge of herbs and healing is not of this world—it is a gift from the devil himself. Their refusal to confess only further proves their guilt."

Eliza, her voice steady despite the fear that gripped her heart, spoke up. "We are healers, not witches. The knowledge we possess has been passed down through generations, a gift from our ancestors, not from the devil. We have never harmed anyone; we have only sought to help those in need."

But her words fell on deaf ears. The crowd, already whipped into a frenzy by Sir Edward and the Witchfinder General, began to murmur, their voices rising in a chorus of condemnation. They had already made up their minds—the sisters were guilty, and they deserved to be punished.

Sir Edward raised his hand, silencing the crowd. "The time for words has passed. The evidence is clear, and the verdict is unanimous. The Blackthorn sisters are hereby condemned to death by hanging, their bodies to be buried in unconsecrated ground, where they will be denied peace in both this world and the next."

The room erupted in cheers and shouts, the villagers celebrating the verdict as if it were a victory. But amidst the chaos, the sisters remained calm, their minds already racing ahead to what would come next. They knew that they would not escape this fate, but they also knew that they would not go quietly.

The sisters stared at Sir Edward, the reality of his words crashing down on them like a tidal wave. The decision was final, their fate sealed by the blind fear and hatred that had once been admiration and respect. The betrayal cut deep, and for a moment, a silence heavy with sorrow hung in the air, thicker than the smoke curling from the Tavern's hearth.

Margaret's hands trembled as she pressed them together in prayer, but her voice quavered with anger and despair. "May God forgive you all," she whispered, though her eyes showed little hope that her plea would be heard. She had been the one who had tended to the sick, who had soothed mothers in labour and whispered prayers over newborns. How had her faith and healing hands brought her here?

Anne could barely hold back her tears, though she fought to keep her voice steady. "You were our neighbours," she said, her voice thick with emotion. "We grew up among you, shared your joys and sorrows. How could you do this to us? We have done nothing wrong. You know this." Her words, filled with the innocence of someone who had always believed in the goodness of people, were met with cold stares. The villagers could not look her in the eye; they turned their gazes away, denying their complicity.

Eliza felt the burden of her sisters' fear and grief as if it were her own. She squared her shoulders and looked at Sir Edward with an intensity that made him flinch ever so slightly. "If you think we are witches," she said, her voice firm and unwavering, "then witches we shall be. Do you want to see darkness in us? You shall have it."

The room, so full of energy just moments before, fell deathly quiet. The sisters had always been the heart of the village—a presence that had brought light and healing. With Eliza's words, the warmth was gone, replaced by something cold and ominous. The crowd shifted uneasily, some looking toward the door as though they had suddenly been trapped in a room with something far more dangerous than they had anticipated.

The guards moved quickly, dragging the sisters to their feet and out of the Tavern, where the night air was sharp and cold. The journey to the blackthorn tree was silent, save for the rattling of chains and the distant roll of thunder. The sky had grown darker, heavy with the promise of a storm, as though the heavens were preparing to mourn the fate of the Blackthorn sisters.

As the villagers dispersed, satisfied with the trial's outcome, the sisters were led out of the Tavern and back into the night. The air was cold, a chill that cut through their thin clothing and seeped into their bones. But the sisters felt no fear—only a deep, burning resolve.

The sisters were taken to a small, decrepit cell on the outskirts of the village, where they would spend their final night. The cell was damp and smelled of rot, a fitting place for those condemned to die. But the sisters did not waste time lamenting their fate. Instead, they huddled together, their voices low as they whispered a plan.

""We cannot let them win," Eliza said, her voice fierce. "They may take our lives, but they cannot take our spirit. We must make them pay for what they have done."

Margaret nodded, her eyes blazing with determination. "We have the power. We can use it, even in death. They will not be rid of us so easily."

Anne spoke last; her voice was soft but unwavering. "I stand by what Eliza said earlier—if they see us as witches, we shall become witches. We will curse this village; every misfortune that strikes will only deepen their fears. They will believe they are cursed, driving them mad."

And so, the sisters made their vow in the dark, cold cell. They would not go quietly into the night. They would curse Blackthorn Hollow, bringing misery and despair to all who had wronged them. They would return, in spirit if not in body, to exact their revenge.

As the night wore on, the sisters began to chant, their voices rising and falling in a rhythm that seemed to echo through the cell walls. They called upon the spirits of their ancestors, upon the earth and sky, upon the power that had always flowed through their veins. They poured all their pain, anger, and fear into the curse, weaving it into a web of dark magic that would spread through the village like a plague.

In the pale light of dawn, the sisters were dragged from their cell and shackled together, their wrists bound with iron chains that bit into their skin. They were then loaded onto the back of a wooden cart, their fate sealed.

The villagers, who had followed the cart from the village, gathered in the clearing, their faces a mixture of grim determination and fear. They had come to witness the execution, to see the Blackthorn sisters meet their end beneath the tree that had stood for centuries, a silent witness to countless sorrows.

As the cart came to a halt beneath the twisted, ancient tree, the sisters were not pulled down but kept aboard as the executioner approached. The nooses were slipped over their heads, rough and biting against their skin. Yet, even at this moment, they were united, their hands clasped together as they stood side by side.

Margaret, her voice trembling with a mixture of fear and defiance, began to chant a prayer, but it soon morphed into something else—something darker. Anne joined her, her voice rising in a powerful harmony that resonated with the surrounding air. Eliza spoke last, her words clear and filled with purpose. "If you believe us to be witches, then witches we shall be. We curse this village and all who have betrayed us. Every misfortune that befalls you, and every shadow that darkens your doors, will be our doing. We will haunt you from this life into the next."

THE EXECUTIONER, HIS face hidden beneath his hood, showed no sign of hesitation. He moved to the horses and drove them forward with a sharp crack of his whip. The cart lurched, and the sisters were left hanging, their bodies twisting in the air as the nooses tightened around their necks. But even as their breath was stolen, they did not stop chanting. Their voices, though strangled and broken, continued to curse the village, to call down retribution on those who had condemned them.

As the last words left their lips, the sky above them erupted. A storm broke out with a fury that seemed otherworldly, lightning cracking through the air like the very wrath of God. Rain poured down in torrents, drenching the village and its people. The wind howled, whipping through the trees and tearing at the clothes of the onlookers, who scattered in fear.

The sisters hung in the air, momentarily twisting and grabbing at the nooses as they tightened around their necks. But even as their breath was stolen, they continued to chant, their voices growing hoarse but unrelenting. The villagers watched in horrified fascination as the sisters' bodies convulsed, their fingers clawing at the ropes in a desperate attempt to free themselves.

And then, as if in response to their final curse, the sky above the blackthorn tree darkened. A storm gathered with unnatural speed, swirling clouds encircling the sisters' heads. Lightning crackled and flashed, illuminating their faces, twisted in agony and defiance. The wind howled through the clearing, whipping the villagers' clothing and stinging their faces with sharp bursts of rain.

A lightning bolt struck the blackthorn tree with one final, deafening crack, sending a shockwave through the ground. The sisters' bodies jerked violently as the ropes snapped taut, and then they went still. But even in death, their curse lingered in the air, a palpable presence that sent a shiver down the spines of all who had gathered to watch.

As the last echoes of their chant faded, the heavens opened, unleashing a torrential downpour. Rain lashed the village of Blackthorn Hollow, soaking the earth and turning the streets into rivers of mud.

Tavern Scene: The Price of Blood

The atmosphere in the Tavern was markedly different from the sombre scene beneath the blackthorn tree. Inside, the warm glow of the firelight flickered off the rough-hewn wooden beams and stone walls. Sir Edward Grantham, John Stearne, and Matthew Hopkins sat around a sturdy oak table, their pewter mugs filled with ale. The weight of what had transpired outside hung in the air, but the men showed no signs of remorse.

Matthew Hopkins took a long draught from his mug, his lips curling into a satisfied smile as he set it down with a clink. "Twenty-three pounds," he said, his voice carrying a note of triumph as he leaned back in his chair. "A fair price for ridding your village of those Blackthorn witches. Business has been good. My book, *The Discovery of Witches*, is selling well, and I am increasingly in demand. From market town to village, I've been swamped ensuring justice is served."

Sir Edward nodded, his expression one of detached satisfaction. He reached into a leather pouch at his side and drew out a small stack of coins. The weight of the silver gleamed dully in the dim light as he slid it across the table toward Hopkins. "Your assistance has been invaluable, Matthew. The good people of Blackthorn Hollow can sleep easier now, thanks to your expertise."

Hopkins picked up the coins, counting them before tucking them away. He raised his mug in a mock toast. "To justice," he said with a smirk, and the other men echoed the sentiment as they drank deeply.

As the ale flowed and the conversation turned to lighter topics, the door to the Tavern creaked open. A man stepped in, his face pale and drawn, a sheaf of documents clutched tightly in his hands. It was the Blackthorn town clerk, a thin, nervous-looking fellow who seemed out of place among the more robust men in the room. He approached Sir Edward with the air of a man who had been coerced into an unpleasant task.

"Sir Edward," the clerk began, his voice trembling slightly as he extended the documents. "As agreed, the deeds to the Blackthorn sisters' land. The transfer has been finalised. It is now yours in payment for ridding the village of the witches."

Sir Edward took the papers with a nod, his eyes gleaming with satisfaction as he scanned the contents. The land had been precious to the sisters—rich with the herbs they had used in their healing practices fertile soil that had sustained them for generations. But now, it was his, a prize won through fear and manipulation.

"Excellent," Sir Edward murmured, folding the documents and slipping them into his coat. "This land will serve me well. It's more valuable than the villagers ever realised. With the witches gone, nothing is standing in my way."

John Stearne, who had remained quiet until now, leaned forward with a sly grin. "It's a good piece of land, Edward. You've done well for yourself."

Sir Edward merely smiled, lifting his mug to his lips. "Indeed. The Blackthorn land will yield much in the years to come. And with the curse of those witches dispelled, Blackthorn Hollow will flourish under my guidance."

Matthew Hopkins chuckled darkly. "A wise investment, Sir Edward. Just be careful. Witches are known to leave behind a legacy, even in death."

Sir Edward waved off the warning with a dismissive gesture. "Superstition, nothing more. The village needed a scapegoat, and now they have it. We'll rebuild; soon enough, no one will remember the Blackthorn sisters or their so-called curse."

The men shared a final round of ale, toasting to their success. But outside, the storm raged on, the wind howling as if the very elements were protesting the injustice that had been done. The blackthorn tree stood tall against the darkened sky, waiting for the day the curse would come to fruition.

Meanwhile, back at the ancient tree, the sisters' bodies hung lifeless from the branches, but their curse had taken root. The storm raged on, circling above the village for seven long days. The villagers, trapped in their homes by the relentless rain and wind, whispered of the curse, the witches they had condemned, and the terrible mistake they had made.

But it was too late. Blackthorn Hollow would never be the same. The land, once fertile and vibrant, began to wither. Crops failed, livestock sickened, and the village slowly fell into decay. The people, haunted by the memory of the Blackthorn sisters and the curse they had unleashed, lived in fear of the dark magic they had tried to destroy. They had wanted witches, and ultimately, they had created them.

Chapter Twelve: Emily Confronts the Past

The rain-soaked landscape of Blackthorn Hollow seemed to echo with the whispers of the past as Emily trudged through the thick mud, her thoughts weighed down by the revelations she had uncovered. The sky was a muted grey, casting the village in a pallor that matched her mood. She was close now—closer than ever to uncovering the truth of the Blackthorn sisters' tragic fate. But with each step she took, she felt the weight of history pressing down on her as if the very ground beneath her feet was urging her to turn back.

Emily had spent weeks sifting through old documents, poring over maps and letters, and piecing together the fragmented history of the sisters. Their story had been buried deep beneath layers of fear, superstition, and deliberate obfuscation. But now, as she stood at the edge of the small, overgrown clearing where the blackthorn tree once stood, she knew she was on the cusp of something monumental.

The clearing was quiet, save for the occasional rustle of leaves in the wind. The blackthorn tree, once the site of the sisters' execution, was now just a twisted, ancient stump, its dark, gnarled roots still gripping the earth like skeletal fingers. It was here, according to her research, that the sisters had been buried in unmarked graves, denied even the dignity of consecrated ground.

As Emily knelt by the stump, brushing away the leaves and debris gathered at its base, she felt a chill run down her spine. The air around her seemed to grow colder, and the light dimmed as though the sun itself was being blotted out. She knew she was not alone.

The first time the sisters' spirits had reached out to her, it had been in her dreams. Their faces had been pale and ghostly, their eyes filled with a sorrow that had haunted Emily even after she awoke. But now, in the fading light of day, she felt their presence more strongly than ever before.

"Emily..." The voice was soft, almost a whisper, but it cut through the silence like a knife. Emily froze, her breath catching in her throat as she slowly turned her head. Standing before her, their forms flickering like the flames of a dying fire, were the Blackthorn sisters.

Eliza, Margaret, and Anne appeared as they had in life, their features delicate and sharp, their eyes dark with the pain of their final moments. But there was something else in their gaze now—something that Emily had not seen before. It was a plea, a desperate, aching need for justice.

"You've come so far," Eliza said, her voice steady despite the ethereal quality of her appearance. "You've uncovered much, but there is still more you must know."

Emily nodded, her voice failing as she took in the sight of the sisters. They were so real and tangible, yet she knew they existed in a space between the living and the dead, caught in a purgatory from which they could not escape.

"Show me," Emily finally managed to whisper. "Show me what I need to know."

The sisters exchanged a glance, and then, as one, they stepped forward, their hands outstretched. Emily felt a surge of cold energy as their fingers brushed against her skin, and suddenly, the world around her shifted.

She was no longer in the clearing. The landscape had changed, morphing into a nightmarish vision of Blackthorn Hollow as it had been on the day of the sisters' trial. The village square was filled with people—men, women, and children—all gathered to witness the spectacle. Emily felt herself being pulled through the crowd, her feet moving of their own accord until she stood at the front, just behind the makeshift courtroom that had been set up in the Tavern.

She watched in horror as the trial played out before her, the accusations, the lies, the manipulation. Sir Edward Grantham sat at the head of the table, his expression one of cold detachment as he listened to the villagers' testimonies. Emily could see the gleam in his eye, the satisfaction he took in their words, as each one condemned the sisters further.

"He wanted our land," Margaret echoed in Emily's mind. "He knew that if we were out of the way, he could take it for himself."

The scene shifted again, and Emily found herself in the dark, damp cell where the sisters had spent their final night. She could feel the cold seeping into her bones and hear the faint water drip as it trickled down the stone walls. The sisters were huddled together, their faces pale and drawn, their eyes filled with fear and determination.

"We did what we had to," Anne said her voice barely a whisper. "We couldn't let him win."

Emily watched as the sisters chanted their curses, their voices growing stronger with each word until the air vibrated with their anger and pain. She could feel the power of their words, the dark magic woven into the fabric of the village, and she knew that this curse had doomed Blackthorn Hollow to its slow, inevitable decline.

But there was more—something else that she needed to understand. The scene shifted again, and Emily stood in a grand, candlelit room. Sir Edward was there, seated at a large oak desk, a quill in his hand as he signed a document. Emily moved closer, her heart pounding as she saw the words on the page. It was a deed transferring the Blackthorn land to Sir Edward's name. The ink was still wet, the seal freshly pressed.

"He had us killed for this," Eliza said, her voice filled with a cold fury. "He used the witch trial as a cover to steal what was ours."

The vision faded, and Emily was back in the clearing, the blackthorn stump looming like a gravestone. The sisters were still there, their faces shadowed in the dim light, but their eyes had a new resolve.

"You know the truth now," Eliza said, her voice strong. "But knowing isn't enough. You must help us find justice."

Emily nodded, her mind racing with everything she had seen. She had to make this right and bring the truth to light, no matter the cost.

But as she turned to leave the clearing, a figure emerged from the shadows. Emily's heart skipped a beat as she recognised the man from the pub who had warned her to stop digging into the past. His face was twisted in anger, his eyes cold and unyielding.

"Trevor Grantham," he said, his voice low and threatening. "You've gone too far, Emily. My family has always taken care of this village, and we're not about to let some outsider ruin everything we've built."

Emily took a step back, her heart pounding in her chest. She had suspected that Trevor was connected to Sir Edward, but seeing him here in this place was almost too much to bear.

"Your ancestor was a murderer," Emily spat, her voice shaking with fury. "He killed those women to steal their land, and you've been reaping the benefits ever since."

Trevor's expression darkened, and he took a step towards her. "You don't know what you're talking about. Those witches got what they deserved, and if you keep pushing, you'll end up just like them."

Emily felt a surge of fear, but she forced herself to stand her ground. "I'm not afraid of you, Trevor. The truth will come out, and when it does, you and your family will be the ones who suffer."

Trevor's eyes narrowed, and for a moment, Emily thought he might strike her. But then, with a sneer, he turned and disappeared back into the shadows, leaving Emily alone with the spirits of the Blackthorn sisters.

The air was tense, but Emily knew what she had to do. She would not be intimidated would not be silenced. The sisters had suffered enough, and it was time for their story to be told.

Emily made her way to the village library, her mind racing with the discoveries she had made. She headed straight for the archives, where the older records and documents were stored. After speaking with the librarian, she was granted access to the vault where the land registry documents were kept.

Carefully, she pulled out the old, yellowed papers, her fingers trembling slightly as she opened them. There it was—Sir Edward Grantham's signature, bold and unmistakable, scrawled at the bottom of the deed that transferred the Blackthorn sisters' land to his name. The ink had faded over the centuries, but the significance of what she held in her hands was as clear as ever.

She sat down at one of the reading tables, her heart pounding as she examined the document in detail. According to some old newspaper cuttings she found on the microfiche, the land had initially been used for growing crops—wheat, barley, and maise. The articles described the land as fertile and productive, vital to the village's agricultural life.

But that was years ago. The more recent articles told a different story. The land had been barren for decades, and its once-rich soil was now cracked and dry. The villagers, steeped in the area's folklore, believed it was the curse of the Blackthorn sisters that had rendered the land useless—a final act of vengeance from beyond the grave.

As the library closed and the last of the evening light faded, Emily gathered her notes and slipped the old documents back into their protective covers. The building was quiet, the usual bustle of the day replaced by the soft rustle of paper and the distant hum of the librarian's activities. Night had fallen by the time she stepped out into the cool air, and the streets of Blackthorn Hollow were bathed in the soft glow of the street lamps, their light casting long shadows on the cobblestone paths.

The walk back to the cottage was peaceful, but Emily's mind was anything but. The more recent articles she had found told a troubling story—one of decay and desolation.

As she approached the cottage, she saw James waiting for her by the window, his silhouette illuminated by the warm light from inside. He turned as she opened the door, his face lighting up with a smile that made her feel instantly at ease.

"Welcome back," James said, stepping forward to take her coat. "You've been gone a while. Did you find what you were looking for?"

Emily nodded, but her expression remained serious. "I did, but it's not good news," she replied, moving to the fireplace to warm her hands. "The land... it's in worse shape than I thought. It's been barren for years, and the villagers think it's because of the curse."

James frowned as he poured her a cup of tea, handing it to her as she settled into a chair by the fire. "The curse again. But there has to be more to it than that, right?"

Emily sipped the tea, feeling the warmth spread through her chilled fingers. "Yes, there is," she said. "The land was barren for so long that the village nearly collapsed. The Granthams, realising they needed to do something, eventually built new houses on it. The cottages they've put up fit in with the village's old-world charm, and now they're used as holiday rentals for tourists as well as homes for some of the villagers."

James raised an eyebrow. "That sounds like it's been good for the village, though. More jobs, more money coming in—what's the problem?"

Emily sighed. "That's exactly why it's such a delicate subject. After the land became barren, the village lost its main sources of income. They used to produce beer and bread, not just for themselves but for the surrounding villages, too. The income from those trades kept the village alive. But when the crops failed, everything fell apart. The villagers who watched the sisters die were left with nothing. Many of them starved or were forced to leave Blackthorn Hollow to find work elsewhere. The village was practically desolate for decades."

James sat down beside her, a thoughtful look on his face. "So, the Granthams came in and built these cottages to revive the village, to replace the lost income."

"Exactly," Emily said, nodding. "But it's more complicated than that. The villagers are still haunted by what happened, even if they don't discuss it openly. They might not believe in the curse, but they know something went terribly wrong after the sisters were killed. And now, with the village making money again, there's a lot of pressure to keep things as they are."

James leaned back, considering her words. "It's no wonder people are touchy about the subject. They're afraid of digging up the past because it could upset the delicate balance they've managed to restore."

"Exactly," Emily agreed. "But I can't help feeling that by avoiding the truth, they're still under the shadow of what happened. The Granthams may have brought the village back from the brink, but the cost of that revival is built on a foundation of lies and injustice."

James reached out and took her hand, giving it a reassuring squeeze. "We'll find a way to bring the truth to light without destroying what's been rebuilt. The village deserves to know its true history, and the Blackthorn sisters deserve justice."

Emily looked at him, feeling both the weight of the responsibility and the comfort of his support. "It's going to be a difficult road," she admitted. "But we owe it to the sisters—and to the village—to uncover the truth, no matter what."

James nodded, his eyes steady and determined. "We're in this together, Emily. Whatever it takes."

Unconvinced by the idea of a supernatural curse, Emily sought a more rational explanation. The fire crackled softly in the hearth, casting a warm glow over the room, but Emily's thoughts were anything but calm. She knew she needed help to make sense of what she had uncovered.

EMILY REACHED FOR THE documents she had spread out on the coffee table. "I found the land registry documents with Sir Edward Grantham's signature."

James looked at the documents, his brow furrowed in thought. "If the land was once fertile but has since deteriorated, it could be due to environmental factors rather than something supernatural," he suggested. "Have you considered the possibility of soil degradation or erosion?"

EMILY'S EYES LIT UP at his suggestion. "I hadn't, but it makes perfect sense. Do you know anyone who might help us figure out what's happened to the soil? A scientist or an expert in this kind of thing?"

James smiled, pleased that he could contribute to her research. "Actually, I do. I worked with a microbiology soil scientist on a project a few years ago—Dr. Claire Donovan. She specialises in land use and soil health. I could contact her and see if she'd be willing to help us."

THAT WOULD BE AMAZING," Emily replied, relief washing over her. "If we can understand what's happened to the land, it might help us see how everything fits together. Maybe Sir Edward's greed didn't just destroy the sisters—it destroyed the land too."

James reached over and squeezed her hand. "We'll get to the bottom of this," he assured her. "And maybe, in doing so, we can finally give the sisters some peace."

The next day, James made contact with Dr. Donovan, who was intrigued by the case and agreed to provide her expertise. Over the phone, she listened carefully as Emily and James described the history of the land and its current barren state.

"This sounds like a classic case of soil and nutrient erosion," Dr. Donovan said thoughtfully. "It's not uncommon in areas where the land has been overworked and improperly managed. The constant tilling and replanting of crops can lead to soil degradation, especially if the land is subjected to heavy rainfall or drought."

"ANNUAL CROPPING," DR. Donovan explained, "requires fields to be periodically cultivated and re-sown as crops are harvested yearly. This constant disturbance of the soil, especially in areas where the land is repeatedly tilled, can result in significant erosion, particularly when heavy rains occur."

Emily nodded as Dr. Donovan spoke. "So, it's possible that the land's infertility is due to years of unsustainable farming practices?" Emily asked.

"Exactly," Dr. Donovan confirmed. "When soil is disturbed too often, it loses its structure, making it more susceptible to erosion. As the topsoil is washed away, it takes with it vital nutrients and any pesticides that have been applied, further degrading the land's fertility. And with the changing climate—more intense rainfall, longer droughts—the problem is only getting worse."

Emily exchanged a look with James. "So, the curse the villagers believe in might actually be the result of environmental damage?"

"In a way, yes," Dr. Donovan replied. "It's not a supernatural curse, but rather the consequence of poor land management and environmental changes. The clay-heavy soils in that area can exacerbate the problem—clay soils tend to dry out quickly during droughts and become waterlogged after heavy rain, making them particularly challenging for farming."

Emily felt a mixture of relief and sadness. "Thank you, Dr. Donovan," she said. "This helps a lot. I think we're finally starting to understand what's really going on."

After the call ended, Emily sat back, her mind spinning with the implications of what they had learned. "It's tragic," she said quietly. "The villagers blamed the sisters for cursing the land, but it was really Sir Edward's greed and the misuse of the land that led to its ruin."

James nodded in agreement. "It just goes to show how easily history can be twisted by fear and superstition. But now that we know the truth, maybe we can do something to help the village—and the sisters."

Emily smiled at him, feeling a renewed sense of purpose. "You're right. This is about more than just uncovering the past—it's about setting things right, for everyone involved."

Together, they began to formulate a plan to present their findings to the villagers and suggest alternative approaches to land management that could restore the fertility of the soil. As they worked, Emily felt the presence of the

Blackthorn sisters lingering nearby, as if watching over them, guiding them toward justice.

Chapter Thirteen: The Final Reckoning

As the biting winter wind swept through the bare branches of the trees in Blackthorn Hollow, Emily Ward stood in the heart of the village, knowing that today would change everything. The weak winter sun barely pierced the thick, grey clouds overhead, casting a cold, muted light over the snow-dusted ground. After countless hours spent in the village library, poring over ancient documents, parish records, and obscure references, Emily had finally uncovered the last piece of evidence she needed to exonerate the Blackthorn sisters and expose the crimes of Sir Edward Grantham.

The discovery had shaken her to her core, but what shocked her even more was the revelation that she was a distant relative of the sisters. This newfound connection made her mission personal—this was her family's story. The knowledge weighed heavily on her, the chill in the air echoing the cold determination she felt within. Today, she would bring the truth to light and seek justice for the sisters who had suffered so long ago.

The Blackthorn sisters—Eliza, Margaret, and Anne—were not just tragic figures from the past. They were kin, their blood running through her veins. The knowledge gave her strength and a purpose that went beyond mere historical curiosity. This was about justice, not only for the sisters but for herself and all the women who had suffered under the weight of baseless accusations and the ruthless grip of power.

After weeks of painstaking research, sleepless nights, and unsettling encounters with the Blackthorn sisters' spirits, Emily finally uncovered the last piece of the puzzle. The evidence she now held in her hands would not only clear the sisters' names but also expose the dark legacy of Sir Edward Grantham. The truth, long buried beneath centuries of fear and superstition, was about to come to light.

Her heart raced as she walked to the village hall, the leather-bound journal clutched tightly in her hands. It contained the damning evidence that would vindicate the sisters and reveal the truth about Sir Edward.

Usually quiet and sombre, the hall buzzed with activity as villagers gathered, their faces mixed with curiosity, anxiety, and anticipation.

Emily could hear the murmurs in the crowd as she approached the front of the hall.

"Did you hear what Emily Ward has uncovered?" one elderly woman whispered to her friend as they walked toward the hall. "They say she's found proof that the Blackthorn sisters were innocent all along."

Her friend nodded, her face lined with concern. "Aye, I've heard. But what does it mean for the village? If Sir Edward really did take the land through false pretences, what will happen to us now?"

Overhearing their conversation, a younger man chimed in, his voice tinged with scepticism. "I'm not sure I believe it. All this talk of curses and spirits—seems like a lot of nonsense to me. But if she has evidence, we should at least hear her out."

Another villager, an older man who had lived in Blackthorn Hollow his entire life, shook his head gravely. "It's not nonsense. I remember my grandfather telling me stories about the sisters and what happened to them. If Emily's found the truth, we owe them to listen."

The crowd's quiet conversation underscored the tension in the room. The villagers had lived with the story of the Blackthorn sisters for generations. It was a tale steeped in mystery and fear, whispered over hearth fires on cold nights, but always with a sense of reverence for the wronged women. Now, with the truth threatening to surface, they faced a reckoning with their past and the responsibility to make amends.

Emily stood before the gathered villagers, her gaze steady, her heart pounding. She took a deep breath, willing herself to remain calm. The words she was about to speak would change everything, not just for her but for the entire village.

Emily knew she had to choose them carefully.

"We need to acknowledge what happened," Emily began, her voice clear and firm, "and then we need to move forward. The Granthams must publicly apologise for the injustices committed against the Blackthorn sisters. It's not enough to simply acknowledge the past—we must right the wrongs that were done. The sisters must be formally pardoned, and their graves, whether they are moved to consecrated ground or blessed where they rest, must be honoured.

The village should take collective ownership of the land, and while much of it has been developed with housing and cottages, we can use what remains and restore it. We must ensure that it becomes productive again for agriculture and as a community resource. Using sustainable practices honouring the sisters' legacy, we can breathe new life into this land and build a future that respects our past."

The room fell silent as the weight of her words settled over the villagers. They had lived with the story of the Blackthorn sisters for generations, but now, they faced the reality of their own history and the responsibility to make amends. Emily could see the uncertainty in their eyes, the fear of what this new knowledge would mean for them, for their future.

After a long pause, an elderly man in the back of the room stood up, his voice firm despite his age. "I've lived in this village my whole life," he said, his gaze sweeping the room. "And I've seen how we've suffered because of the lies we were told. It's time we set things right. I, for one, am ready to do whatever it takes."

His words broke the tension in the room. Slowly, others began to nod in agreement, their expressions shifting from fear to resolve. The truth, it seemed, had finally found its place in Blackthorn Hollow, and with it, the village had a chance to heal.

As the villagers absorbed the weight of Emily's revelations, a sense of solidarity began to take root among them. They spoke in hushed tones about the land's potential, imagining how it could be restored and repurposed. Once symbols of a painful legacy, the cottages and houses that the Granthams had built could be transformed into homes for those who wished to stay and work the land. The villagers discussed the possibility of creating a community garden. In this space, everyone could contribute and benefit from the fruits of their labour, just as the Blackthorn sisters had once tended their gardens for the good of all.

The energy in the room shifted from one of tension to one of hope. Emily watched as the villagers, divided by old grudges and fears, began to come together. They were no longer just individuals trying to survive in a cursed village; they were a community with a shared goal, history, and a shared future.

After the presentation, Emily led the villagers to the clearing where the ancient blackthorn tree once stood. The atmosphere was heavy with anticipation as she prepared a ritual to free the spirits of the Blackthorn sisters and lift the curse that had plagued the village for centuries.

The clearing was a sombre place, marked by the remnants of the tree that had once been the centre of so much suffering. Its twisted roots still clung to the earth, a reminder of the Blackthorn sisters' deep ties to the land. Emily had spent days preparing for this moment, gathering the necessary elements for the ritual that would finally bring peace to the sisters' restless spirits.

Kneeling by the stump of the blackthorn tree, Emily sprinkled a mixture of soil from the sisters' graves and seeds from the tree itself around the stump, symbolising renewal and justice. The dark and rich soil held the weight of centuries of injustice, while the seeds represented the potential for a new life, a chance to grow beyond the pain of the past.

"We are here to honour Eliza, Margaret, and Anne Blackthorn," she began, her voice steady. "Their lives were unjustly taken, but today we set things right."

As she spoke, a breeze stirred, carrying her words through the clearing. The villagers watched in reverent silence, understanding that this moment marked the end of a dark chapter in their history. The air was thick with the presence of the past, the weight of the sisters' suffering palpable in the quiet of the clearing.

Emily reached into her pocket and pulled out a small, weathered locket. Her family passed it down, symbolising their connection to the Blackthorn sisters. Inside was a lock of hair, said to belong to Eliza Blackthorn, the eldest of the sisters. Holding the locket in her hand, Emily whispered a prayer for the sisters' souls, asking for their forgiveness and blessing.

She placed the locket at the base of the stump, a final offering to the spirits that had haunted the village for so long. As she did, the breeze intensified, swirling around the clearing lifting leaves and dust into the air. The villagers gasped as the wind grew stronger, tugging at their clothes and hair.

For a moment, it seemed as though the very earth was responding to Emily's actions. The ground trembled slightly, and a low hum filled the air, like the distant echo of silenced voices. The villagers stood frozen, their eyes wide with fear and wonder.

Then, just as suddenly as it had begun, the wind died down, leaving the clearing in an eerie stillness. The hum faded into silence, and the tension in the air dissipated. The villagers looked around, unsure of what had just happened, but feeling a sense of release, as though a great weight had been lifted from their shoulders.

Emily stood, her heart pounding in her chest. She knew that the ritual had worked. The Blackthorn sisters' spirits had been set free, their curse lifted from the village. The clearing, once a place of pain and sorrow, now felt different—lighter, almost serene.

The villagers began to stir, talking quietly among themselves, their voices filled with a mix of relief and disbelief. They had witnessed something extraordinary, something beyond their understanding, but they knew, deep down, that the curse that had plagued their village for so long was finally over.

But the sense of peace that settled over the clearing did not reach everyone.

In his grand estate, Sir Trevor Grantham paced angrily in his study, his gaze fixed on the village below through the large window. He could see the villagers gathering in small groups, discussing Emily Ward's findings. The news had reached him quickly, and he knew that if Emily succeeded in revealing the truth, everything his family had built on stolen land would crumble.

His solicitor had warned him of the potential fallout, but Sir Trevor's pride and greed overwhelmed his better judgment. He clenched his fists, his knuckles turning white as he imagined the scene unfolding in the village hall. "I won't let that witch destroy everything my family has built!" he snarled, slamming his fist on the desk.

Sir Trevor knew that legally, the land was secure in his possession. The laws of the 21st century were on his side—statutes of limitations, adverse possession, and the doctrine of laches all protected his claim. No court would entertain a claim for land taken over three centuries ago, especially not one based on accusations of witchcraft and deceit from the distant past.

But the law was one thing; the will of the people was another. Sir Trevor understood that if the villagers turned against him, if they rallied behind Emily and demanded restitution, his hold on the land could become precarious. He couldn't afford to let that happen. He needed to act, and he needed to act swiftly.

No, he would not stand idly by. He would find a way to crush this uprising, to silence Emily once and for all. He would remind the villagers of their place, of the power the Granthams held over them. If he couldn't use the law to protect his land, he would use fear.

Sir Trevor's thoughts turned dark as he contemplated his next move. He had connections, people who owed him favours, who could be persuaded to deal with this problem discreetly. Perhaps a fire in the village library would destroy the evidence Emily had gathered. Or an "accident" could be arranged, something that would remove Emily from the equation permanently.

As he considered these options, a cold, calculating smile spread across his face. He would stop at nothing to protect his legacy, to ensure that the Grantham name remained untarnished. The villagers might think they could rise against him, but they were fools if they believed they could win.

His hatred for Emily festered into something dark and vindictive. He could still hear the echoes of their last encounter in his mind. When Emily confronted him with the evidence, he spat venomous words at her, his voice dripping with contempt.

"You're nothing but a witch," he had hissed, leaning in close. "If this were the old days, you'd be burned at the stake just like your ancestors. I wish I could see you swing from the same tree they hanged from."

But Emily had met his gaze with unwavering resolve, unshaken by his threats. She knew that Sir Trevor's words were the last desperate acts of a man whose power was slipping away, and his cruel fantasies only made her more determined to see justice done.

Now, as he watched the villagers from the window of his estate, Sir Trevor's heart burned with rage. He could feel the weight of their judgment pressing in on him. The walls of his ancestral home seemed to close in as the truth crept closer. But deep down, he knew there was no stopping it. Yet, he was determined to give it his all to do just that.

Driven by desperation and fear of losing everything, Sir Trevor resolved to fight to the bitter end. He would not let Emily Ward or anyone else take what was rightfully his. If they wanted a battle, he would give them one.

He stormed out of his study, his footsteps echoing through the grand hallways of his ancestral home. The walls seemed to close in on him, the shadows lengthening as the sun dipped below the horizon. He could feel the weight of the past pressing down on him, the sins of his ancestors haunting every corner of the estate.

As he reached the front door, he paused, his hand on the doorknob. The estate had always been a symbol of his family's power, a testament to their control over the land and the people of Blackthorn Hollow. But now, it felt more like a prison, its grandeur tainted by the knowledge of how it had been acquired.

Sir Trevor shook off the feeling and yanked the door open. He stepped out into the cool evening air, the chill doing little to calm his fury. He needed to stop Emily before she could do any more damage. His mind raced, searching for a way to regain control, to silence her once and for all.

But as he made his way toward the village, something strange began to happen. The path that had always been so familiar to him now seemed foreign, the trees and bushes twisting into unnatural shapes, their branches reaching out like skeletal hands.

Sir Trevor's pace quickened, his breath coming in short gasps as he pushed forward. But the landscape around him continued to shift and change, warping into a nightmarish version of the village he had known all his life. The houses loomed larger, their windows dark and empty, like eyes watching his every move.

The wind whipped around him, tearing at his clothes and hair as the whispers grew into a deafening roar. The voices of the Blackthorn sisters seemed to surround him, their presence pressing in on him from all sides.

"Thief... liar... murderer..."

The accusations echoed through his mind, each word a dagger plunging into his heart. He stumbled, his vision blurring as the path twisted beneath his feet. The ground seemed to shift and buckle, and he fell to his knees, his hands sinking into the cold, damp earth.

Sir Trevor screamed, a sound of pure terror and desperation. But the voices only grew louder, their condemnation echoing in his mind. He clutched his head, his thoughts unravelling as the world around him twisted into chaos.

And then, as suddenly as it had begun, it stopped.

The wind died down, the voices faded, and the world around him returned to normal. Sir Trevor pushed himself up from the ground, his face twisted with fury rather than fear. His heart pounded with a dark resolve, every thought consumed by a burning desire for revenge. He wasn't shaken by guilt or remorse—those emotions were foreign to him. Instead, the humiliation of being brought low by Emily and the villagers fueled his anger. How dare they challenge him, a Grantham, in his own domain?

Wiping the dirt from his clothes, Sir Trevor's mind raced with plans to crush Emily Ward and anyone who dared to support her. He would not rest until he had reclaimed his power and made them all pay. The idea of using the old, twisted stories of the Blackthorn curse didn't seem like nonsense to him anymore—it could be his weapon. He would twist the fear and superstition still lurking in the hearts of the villagers, turning it against Emily, making her the real enemy.

As he stormed back to his estate, his footsteps echoed with determination. There was no guilt, no fear—only the cold, calculating mind of a man bent on vengeance.

Chapter Fourteen: Epilogue - A New Beginning

Emily Ward sat quietly at her desk, surrounded by the comforting clutter of books, papers, and research notes. The soft hum of activity in the university hallway barely penetrated the walls of her office, where the only sound was the faint rustle of pages as she flipped through her manuscript. The late afternoon sun filtered through the tall windows, casting a warm, golden glow over the room. Outside, students and faculty bustled about, but Emily's mind was far from the academic world she had returned to.

Blackthorn Hollow. The small village had left a deep imprint on her soul. It was where she had uncovered the truth about her ancestors, the Blackthorn sisters, and exposed the dark secrets of Sir Edward Grantham's crimes. The village, once gripped by fear and superstition, had begun to heal, and Emily had found herself more connected to it than ever before.

She leaned back in her chair, her thoughts drifting back to her final days in Blackthorn Hollow. Though the events there were now behind her, their impact lingered. The book she had worked on for so long—*The Witches of Blackthorn Hollow: Truth and Injustice in 17th Century Essex*—was finally complete. Soon, it would be published, bringing the story of the Blackthorn sisters to a wider audience and ensuring their legacy endured.

But the book was more than just a scholarly achievement; it was a personal mission fulfilled. For so long, the sisters' stories had been buried under layers of myth and fear, their names tarnished by false accusations of witchcraft. Emily had uncovered the truth, not just for history's sake, but because she knew it was her duty—a responsibility that came with being their descendant.

She thought of the clearing in Blackthorn Hollow where the ancient blackthorn tree had once stood, its gnarled branches a testament to the sisters' strength and resilience. That spot had been transformed into a place of healing and renewal, just as the village itself was undergoing a rebirth. The villagers had rallied together, united by a shared goal: to restore the land and honour the memory of the Blackthorn sisters.

In the weeks following her return to the university, Emily continued to work closely with the villagers, guiding them as they implemented sustainable farming practices to ensure the land's future prosperity. The cottages and housing that the Granthams had built were being repurposed and transformed into homes for those who wished to stay and work the land. The idea of a village cooperative had taken root, and the once-divided community was now coming together to rebuild not just the land but the very fabric of their lives.

The cottage that had once been a place of haunting had become a symbol of healing and history. Emily had taken up residence there for a time, finding solace in its quiet, rustic charm. She had spent hours by the hearth, sifting through old records and documents, piecing together the story that had been hidden for so long. Once filled with the spirits of the past, the cottage was now a place of peace.

Oblivious to the dark plans forming in Sir Trevor's mind, Emily was focused on her work, preparing for the publication of her book and continuing her research on the history of Blackthorn Hollow. The village had become more than just a subject of study for her; it was a place where she had found a sense of belonging, a connection to her ancestors that she had never known before.

She thought often of the last time she had visited the site of the sisters' graves. The unmarked and neglected plot where they had been buried was now a place of reverence and peace. The villagers had come together to erect a simple yet poignant memorial, a stone monument inscribed with the names of Eliza, Margaret, and Anne Blackthorn, along with the words: "In Memory of the Innocent. May They Rest in Peace."

It was a small gesture but one that carried immense weight. For centuries, the sisters had been wrongfully accused, their names stained by the accusations of witchcraft. Now, at last, they were being honoured as the healers and wise women they had always been. The local vicar, moved by the events that had unfolded, had offered to bless the earth where the sisters were buried. The ceremony had been a solemn occasion attended by the entire village.

The villagers had gathered in a procession, walking together to the site of the sisters' graves. The vicar had spoken of forgiveness and reconciliation, asking for peace for the Blackthorn sisters' souls and the village that had wronged them. As he sprinkled holy water over the graves, the villagers stood silently, their heads bowed respectfully. It was a moment of collective catharsis, a final acknowledgement of the past and a commitment to ensuring that such a tragedy would never be repeated.

Emily had stood among them, feeling the weight of the moment and the sisters' presence, no longer in restless spirits but finally at peace. The seeds she had planted in the clearing where the blackthorn tree once stood had begun to sprout, and soon, new blackthorn trees would grow, their branches reaching toward the sky—a living testament to the sisters' resilience.

She found solace in the knowledge that she had played a part in restoring justice and healing Blackthorn Hollow. Once mired in darkness, the village was filled with hope for the future.

But in the shadows, Sir Trevor Grantham was preparing to ensure this new beginning would be far more treacherous than Emily could ever imagine.

Weeks passed, and the village of Blackthorn Hollow continued to thrive. The cooperative that Emily had helped establish was flourishing, and the land was beginning to yield crops again. The villagers had embraced the new practices, using sustainable methods to restore the soil and bring life back to the fields.

Emily made frequent trips to the village, overseeing the progress and offering guidance where needed. She had become a trusted figure among the villagers, someone they looked to for advice and support. The bonds she had formed with them were strong, built on a shared history and a commitment to preserving the legacy of the Blackthorn sisters.

The cottage where Emily had stayed during her time in the village had also been transformed. It was no longer a place of haunting but a symbol of healing and history. The villagers had worked together to restore it, planting a garden filled with herbs and flowers that the sisters had once used in their healing practices. The cottage had become a place of pilgrimage for those who wished to learn about the village's history and pay their respects to the Blackthorn sisters.

Inside, Emily had set up a small museum displaying the artefacts and documents she had uncovered during her research. The walls were lined with photographs, drawings, and maps, each telling a piece of the story that had been hidden for so long. Visitors came from near and far to see the collection, drawn by the tale of the Blackthorn sisters and the village that had wronged them.

But even as the village flourished, a darkness lingered on the horizon.

Sir Trevor Grantham sat brooding in his grand estate, the weight of his family's history pressing down on him like a vice. From the large windows of his study, he could see the village below, the lights flickering as night fell. The village, once under the firm control of the Grantham family, had slipped through his fingers, and the thought filled him with a burning rage.

HE HAD WATCHED WITH growing anger as the villagers gathered to support Emily Ward, their loyalty shifting away from the Grantham name. The idea that a woman—an outsider, no less—had come into his domain and turned the village against him was intolerable. Sir Trevor was a man of deep-seated misogyny, convinced that women were inferior and had no place in positions of power or influence. The fact that Emily had succeeded in uncovering the truth about his ancestors and exposing their crimes only fueled his hatred.

Sir Trevor plotted his revenge as he sat in the dimly lit study with a glass of brandy in hand. He was not easily defeated and would only rest once he had reclaimed his power and destroyed Emily Ward. His thoughts grew darker with each passing moment, his mind consumed by a desire for vengeance.

He had already begun to discredit her work, using his connections to plant doubts about the validity of her research. Rumours had started to spread, whispering that Emily's findings were sensationalist fiction designed to tarnish the Grantham name. He knew people in high places who owed him favours and could be persuaded to publicly question the legitimacy of her work.

But discrediting her research was only the beginning. Sir Trevor wanted to see Emily suffer, to strip her of everything she had gained. He imagined her being driven out of Blackthorn Hollow, out of academia, out of her own life. He fantasised about seeing her reduced to nothing, her reputation in ruins, her spirit broken.

The more he thought about it, the more he became convinced that fear was his greatest weapon. The villagers had always been superstitious, their minds easily swayed by talk of curses and spirits. He would use that to his advantage, twisting the fear and superstition still lurking in their hearts and turning it against Emily. He would make her the real enemy responsible for the village's troubles.

Sir Trevor Grantham had not been idle. His campaign to discredit Emily's work was well underway, and the rumours he had spread were beginning to take hold. In academic circles, whispers of doubt began to circulate—questions about her sources' authenticity and the accuracy of her research. Articles appeared in obscure journals, written by experts who claimed that Emily's findings were based on speculation rather than fact.

Emily was aware of the growing whispers but refused to be swayed. She knew her work was sound, grounded in extensive research and supported by historical evidence. But the doubts planted by Sir Trevor were like a poison, slowly spreading through the academic community.

The villagers, too, began to feel the effects of Sir Trevor's campaign. Strange things started to happen—crops that had been flourishing suddenly withered and died, animals fell ill for no apparent reason, and there were reports of weird noises and sightings near the clearing where the blackthorn tree once stood.

Fear began to creep back into the village, the old superstitions that had once gripped the villagers' hearts resurfacing. Whispers of a curse began circulating, fueled by Sir Trevor's subtle manipulations. The villagers, who had once been united in their efforts to restore the land, began to turn on one another, their newfound solidarity unravelling.

Emily knew that something was wrong, that their progress was being threatened by forces beyond their control. She suspected Sir Trevor was behind the strange occurrences but had no proof. She could only watch as the village she had come to love began to fall apart.

One night, as Emily sat alone in the cottage, she heard a knock at the door. When she opened it, she found an elderly villager standing on the doorstep, his face lined with worry.

"Miss Ward," he said, his voice trembling, "I don't know who else to turn to. There's something dark at work in the village. People are afraid—afraid that the curse has returned."

Emily invited him in, offering him a cup of tea as he sat at the kitchen table. She listened as he spoke of the strange events that had been happening, the fear that was spreading through the village like wildfire.

"I don't believe in curses," the man said, his hands shaking as he wrapped them around the warm mug. "But something's not right. The land was healing, and now it's withering again. The people are scared, Miss Ward. They think the Blackthorn sisters' curse is coming back."

Emily's heart sank. She knew that fear was a powerful force, one that could undo all the progress they had made. But she also knew that the real curse on Blackthorn Hollow was not supernatural—it was the legacy of hatred and greed that had been passed down through generations of the Grantham family.

As the villager left, Emily made a decision. She would not allow Sir Trevor to destroy what they had worked so hard to build. She would fight back, using the truth as her weapon. She would continue to tell the story of the Blackthorn sisters to honour their memory and ensure that their legacy endured.

In the following days, Emily threw herself into her work with renewed determination. She spoke with the villagers, reassuring them that the strange occurrences were not a sign of a curse but of something more mundane—perhaps sabotage. She encouraged them to stand strong, hold on to their progress, and not let fear dictate their actions.

She also gathered evidence of Sir Trevor's involvement in the campaign against her. It was difficult—he was careful, leaving little trace of his actions—but Emily was determined. She reached out to her contacts in the academic world, asking them to watch for any signs of manipulation or false information being spread.

Slowly, the tide began to turn. The villagers, reassured by Emily's calm resolve, began to resist the fear that had gripped them. They returned to work, tending the land and caring for their animals. The cooperative began to function again, and the crops, which had withered, started to recover.

Emily's efforts in the academic world also began to bear fruit. She exposed the false articles for what they were—baseless attacks orchestrated by those interested in discrediting her work. Initially swayed by rumours, her colleagues began to see the truth and rallied to her support.

But Sir Trevor was not finished. He knew his campaign to discredit Emily had failed, and his anger grew each day. The idea that a woman had bested him, that she had not only uncovered the truth about his family's dark past but had also managed to defeat his attempts to destroy her, was intolerable.

He decided that it was time for more drastic measures. If he couldn't destroy Emily's reputation or frighten the villagers into submission, he would find another way to eliminate her.

Late one evening, as Emily sat by the fire in the cottage, she heard a noise outside. It was faint at first, barely audible over the crackling of the flames, but it grew louder—a rustling in the bushes, the sound of footsteps crunching on the gravel path.

She stood up, her heart pounding in her chest. The cottage was isolated, surrounded by fields and woods, and she knew that no one would be coming to visit her at this hour. She reached for the poker by the fireplace, gripping it tightly as she moved toward the door.

The footsteps stopped just outside the door, and for a moment, there was silence. Emily held her breath, her mind racing. She knew that Sir Trevor was capable of anything and would stop at nothing to get what he wanted.

The door burst open, and Sir Trevor stood on the threshold, his face twisted with fury. He lunged at her, his hands outstretched, but Emily was ready. She swung the poker with all her strength, striking him across the shoulder. He stumbled back, cursing, but he quickly recovered and came at her again.

They struggled, and the small cottage suddenly felt smaller as they fought. Sir Trevor was strong, but Emily was determined. She managed to land another blow, this time to his head, and he fell to the floor, unconscious.

Emily stood over him, her chest heaving with exertion, the poker still clutched in her hand. She knew that this was only the beginning, that Sir Trevor would not stop until he had destroyed her. But she also knew that she could not do this alone.

She ran to the door and called out into the night, hoping that anyone would hear her. The village was not far, and she knew the villagers would come to her aid if they knew she was in danger.

Sure enough, within minutes, she heard the sound of voices and saw the glow of lanterns approaching. The villagers arrived, and a small group was led by the same elderly man who had come to her for help just days before.

They found Sir Trevor lying on the floor of the cottage, unconscious but alive. The villagers looked at him with a mix of anger and pity, knowing that he was a man who had been consumed by his own hatred and greed.

In the following days, Sir Trevor Grantham was taken away, his estate seized by the authorities, and his influence over Blackthorn Hollow finally broken. The villagers, relieved to be free of his tyranny, turned their attention back to the future, determined to rebuild their lives and their community.

Emily remained in Blackthorn Hollow for some time. She knew the path ahead would not be easy, but she also knew they had the strength to overcome whatever challenges lay ahead.

The blackthorn trees that Emily had planted continued to grow, their branches reaching toward the sky, a living testament to the resilience of the Blackthorn sisters and the village that had finally found peace.

Emily felt a deep sense of satisfaction as she stood by the memorial one last time. The story of the Blackthorn sisters had been told, their names cleared, and their legacy restored. Blackthorn Hollow had been given a second chance, and Emily knew she had found her place in its future.

The final reckoning had come, and with it, a new beginning. Emily knew there would still be challenges ahead, but she felt a sense of peace for the first time. The sisters' story had been told, and now it was time for the village to write a new chapter built on truth, justice, and hope for the future.

Don't miss out!

Visit the website below and you can sign up to receive emails whenever Samantha Hill publishes a new book. There's no charge and no obligation.

https://books2read.com/r/B-A-PVXIC-LHRWE

BOOKS2READ

Connecting independent readers to independent writers.